I was embarrass....

I was on my way to the cafeteria when I heard this big roar of laughter. There was a group of kids standing outside the cafeteria door. And when I got closer, I saw what was causing the commotion.

Hanging from the doorknob was a forlorn-looking furry object. My heart sank.

That's right. You guessed it.

A toupee.

Jessica and Lila were whooping and dancing around it like a couple of Apaches, and making jokes about scalping the principal.

"They did it," Ellen shouted gleefully. "They got into Mr. Clark's office and snatched it. But they had to do it together so I guess the dare war still isn't over."

Lila and Jessica high-fived each other.

I looked away. I didn't think it was funny at all anymore. I was just opening my mouth to tell them so when I heard this horrible sound.

It was the sound of a throat being cleared.

Everybody heard it at the same time. One by one, every face registered shock—and then fear. Ellen's face went white and Mary's eyes got huge.

Slowly, painfully, we all turned and saw something I'd never expected to see in my whole life.

Mr. Clark—*bald!*

THE UNICORN CLUB

SAVE THE UNICORNS!

Written by
Alice Nicole Johansson

Created by
FRANCINE PASCAL

BANTAM BOOKS
NEW YORK • TORONTO • LONDON • SYDNEY • AUCKLAND

To Molly Jessica W. Wenk

RL 4, 008-012

SAVE THE UNICORNS!
A Bantam Book / January 1994

*Sweet Valley High® and The Unicorn Club™ are
trademarks of Francine Pascal*

Conceived by Francine Pascal

*Produced by Daniel Weiss Associates, Inc.
33 West 17th Street
New York, NY 10011*

Cover art by James Mathewuse

ISBN: 0-553-48202-5

Published simultaneously in the United States and Canada

Bantam Books are published by Bantam Books, a division of Bantam
Doubleday Dell Publishing Group, Inc. Its trademark, consisting of the
words "Bantam Books" and the portrayal of a rooster, is Registered in
U.S. Patent and Trademark Office and in other countries. Marca
Registrada. Bantam Books, 1540 Broadway, New York, New York 10036.

PRINTED IN THE UNITED STATES OF AMERICA

OPM   0 9 8 7 6 5 4 3 2 1

One

I knew seventh grade was going to be fun, but I had this nervous feeling in my stomach about it. I'd had it for two weeks. Ever since school started.

It was the feeling that there were all sorts of things I was supposed to know now that I was in seventh grade—but didn't.

I guess I felt confused and a little intimidated. After all, nobody expects you to know anything when you're in sixth grade. You're just a sixth grader. When you're in the seventh grade, it's different.

Oh, sure, it's not as stressful as being an eighth grader. But no doubt about it, when you hit seventh grade, the pressure is on.

You'd think as a member of the Unicorn Club I would be totally confident. The Unicorns are considered the prettiest and most popular girls at

Sweet Valley Middle School. When I was invited to be a member last year, I was the happiest girl in Sweet Valley, California. *Look out, world, here comes Mandy Miller* was my attitude.

Now my attitude was *Look out, Mandy Miller, here comes the world.*

Maybe I was feeling that way because Janet Howell had graduated from Sweet Valley Middle School and was now in ninth grade at Sweet Valley High. Janet Howell had been the president of the Unicorns for three years in a row.

Not that Janet is my favorite person in the world. She's really bossy and a big know-it-all. (Don't tell her I said that.) But it was nice having somebody older and wiser in charge of things.

Now that she was gone, the Unicorn Club didn't have a president. Without a president we had no direction. No identity. No guidance. No leader.

But you can be sure there were plenty of members interested in the part. We aren't known for our tiny egos.

It didn't take long for Jessica Wakefield and Lila Fowler to propose themselves as presidential candidates. And that's why on this sunny fall afternoon, all the Unicorns were sitting around the Wakefield living room having an emergency meeting. We needed to pick a president.

I loved being in the Wakefields' house. The living room is large and sunny, and all the furniture is done in different tones of green and yellow. There's a sliding glass door that separates the room from the backyard, where red and yellow flowers are planted in the beds on the other side of the swimming pool. Being in the Wakefield living room is like sitting in a garden. It has that designer touch, if you know what I mean. I guess it's because Mrs. Wakefield is a designer. Mrs. Wakefield, by the way, is Jessica and Elizabeth's mom. And I guess you're probably wondering who Elizabeth is, too.

Let's stop for a couple of minutes and let me fill you in a little on who's who.

Jessica Wakefield is my best friend. She has long sun-streaked blond hair and blue-green eyes, and she's really, really pretty. Her sister, Elizabeth, looks exactly like her. They're identical twins. The only way most people can tell them apart is by their hair. Jessica always wears hers in loose waves around her shoulders, and Elizabeth mostly wears hers pulled back in a ponytail or barrettes.

But even though they look alike, they're as different as night and day. You'll see what I mean when you meet them.

What can I say about Jessica? When you're around her, exciting things happen. Exciting good. And exciting bad. You never quite know what Jessica's getting you into until you're in it, and then it's too late. But trust me, life with Jessica is never boring.

Elizabeth, her twin sister, is really smart and talented and a good student—but I like her anyway. (Ha ha!) She was asked to join the Unicorn Club last year but she turned them down. I can understand why. Cool as they are, the Unicorns do spend an awful lot of time talking about boys and makeup and who's popular and stuff like that. Those things aren't very important to Elizabeth.

Actually, they're not as important to me anymore, either. Maybe it's because I'm getting older and maturing, but I'm finding I like to read more than I like to watch TV. I like to talk about current events sometimes instead of boys. And even though I adore talking about makeup and clothes, I don't necessarily think that the way a person looks is all that important.

At that moment I could see Elizabeth and Maria Slater through the sliding glass door of the Wakefields' living room. They were outside in the pool, and I couldn't help thinking it would be fun if they were Unicorns this year. Mostly because they're both really good friends of mine. But also because the Unicorn Club was going to need some new blood this year.

Janet wasn't the only member who had moved on to high school. Tamara Chase and Grace Oliver were in ninth grade this year, too. Grace is only thirteen, but she's such a good student she skipped eighth grade. Kimberly Haver moved to Atlanta with her family at the beginning of the summer, and Belinda Layton switched to a private school called the Lovett Academy, which is about a half hour away. We still hang out with her sometimes, and she still plays Sweet Valley Little League softball.

The Unicorn Club was down to five members: Jessica, Lila Fowler, Mary Wallace, Ellen Riteman, and me. We were an awesome group, even if we were small.

At the moment we were all listening to Lila Fowler talk about the direction we should be moving in as a club. Lila Fowler has brown eyes and long brown hair, which she's always flipping over her shoulder.

Jessica sat in the big wing chair in the Wakefields' living room drinking a soda. Her foot wiggled impatiently and she kept rolling her eyes.

Jessica did that a lot when Lila Fowler was talking. Jessica and Lila are good friends but they're incredibly competitive, and Lila has a slight tendency to brag. OK, fine. A huge tendency to brag.

Lila's bragging drives Jessica crazy, and sometimes it drives me crazy, too. But I have to admit, if I were Lila I'd probably brag a lot. Lila's father is the wealthiest man in town, and Lila's lifestyle is incredibly glamorous. She gets driven around town in a Rolls Royce. Can you believe that? Her parents are divorced, and her mom lives in Europe. Mr. Fowler feels guilty about Lila's not having a mom, so he buys her everything she wants to make it up to her.

Lila's got every single thing in the world a person could want. And her wardrobe is *fabulous*. Today she had on a pair of green washed-silk pants with a matching vest over this gorgeous white, gauzy blouse. I couldn't even imagine what an outfit like that would cost. Probably more than I'm going to spend on my college education.

". . . and if I'm president," Lila was saying, "we can have our meetings at my house. In fact, my father would probably let me remodel the pool house and paint it purple. Then it could be the permanent Unicorn Club headquarters."

(Purple, by the way, is our official club color. All of us try to wear something purple every day—a T-shirt, a sweater, socks, or a ribbon.)

"But we've always taken turns having the meetings at our houses," Mary Wallace said. "That way, everybody gets a turn and nobody has the responsibility of doing it every time." Mary is in eighth grade and has long curly blond hair and gray eyes. She's tall and slim and dresses kind of preppy— lots of oxford shirts and khaki pants.

"I don't mind the responsibility," Lila said quickly.

Mary shook her head. "I don't think my mom would go for that plan. She would say we were taking advantage of you and your dad."

Ellen Riteman and I nodded. I liked having the club meetings at my house. My whole family liked it. My mom says there's nothing better than a big group of giggling girls to make a house feel like a home. And I know Archie, my little brother, likes the Unicorns, even though he won't come right out and admit it. When they come over they pay lots of attention to him and pretend to be afraid of his pet iguana, which really makes him laugh.

Actually, I should have said *most* of my family likes having the club meetings. My sister, Cecelia, is in high school, and she's not too crazy about the Unicorns. But that's because she's completely serious and never does anything wrong or bad or stupid. Needless to say, she and I have nothing in common. I call her Saint Cecelia.

Lila bit her lip, as though she was trying to think of some other reason why she should be president. Finally, she sat up straighter and lifted her chin. "Janet Howell was the president of this club for three years," she said. "And as Janet's first cousin, I think I'm the best person to step into her shoes."

Mary Wallace always makes this motorboat noise when she's trying not to laugh but can't help it. She was making it now and a couple of other people were laughing, too. "The presidency of the Unicorn Club isn't the throne of England," Mary said. "You don't have a hereditary claim on it just because you're Janet's cousin."

Lila tightened her lips and sat back on the sofa. "Then how are we going to pick a president?"

"We could hold elections," I suggested. "You want to be president. And Jessica wants to be president. Maybe we should put our heads down and vote."

"I've got a better idea," Mary said with a mischievous smile. "We could pick a president the same way we pick our members. Candidates for membership have to accept dares. Right? So why not pick a president the same way?"

Everybody began to laugh and applaud.

"All right!" Jessica said, pumping her fist in the air. "A dare war!"

"Now *that's* the kind of thinking that separates the Unicorns from the Chess Club," I said, laughing.

Mary hopped up out of the wing chair, grabbed her notebook, and ripped out two pages. She handed one to Lila and one to Jessica. "You two write down your dares. Writing them down makes them official. Then give them to Mandy to read."

Lila smiled a little, then she began to scribble.

Jessica did the same thing, and then both girls handed me the folded pieces of paper.

"Are the dares all in?" I asked in a deep voice, like a game-show host.

"The dares are in," Jessica and Lila both said in deep voices.

I grinned and opened the first one. "Jessica Wakefield hereby officially dares Lila Fowler to . . . *go into the boys' bathroom after second period tomorrow and put mousse in her hair!*"

"Oooooohhh," the whole group said. Mary and Ellen collapsed on the sofa in giggles.

I noticed that Lila wasn't laughing. And when I opened the next piece of paper, I saw why. "Lila Fowler hereby officially dares Jessica Wakefield to . . . *hide Mr. Swenson's chalk.*"

"Lame!" Ellen cried.

"Bogus!" Mary shouted.

"That hardly counts as a dare at all," Ellen said. "It's too easy."

"Let's do the dares over so that they're more even," Mary suggested. "Going into the boys' bathroom is a lot more embarrassing than getting caught stealing Mr. Swenson's chalk."

"That's not the way it works," Jessica argued. "Once the dares are made, they're official. They stand."

Lila cleared her throat and stood. "Jessica's right. A dare is a dare and a deal is a deal."

"Then let the dare war begin!" Mary shouted.

"I feel a little weird being in seventh grade, too," Elizabeth Wakefield told me later that afternoon.

The meeting was over, and Jessica and I were in the Wakefields' backyard with Elizabeth and Maria drinking sodas by the pool.

"What do you mean you feel weird being in the seventh grade?" Maria asked.

Elizabeth gave a little shrug. "I can see already that I'm not going to be as busy as I was last year. Last year I was editor-in-chief of *The Sixers*, and that took up a lot of my time. I'll be working as a reporter for the *7 & 8 Gazette*, but the eighth graders have most of the really important jobs. I feel like . . ." She shrugged again and then smiled. "I feel like a pea rattling around in a great big pan with a thousand other peas. Not sure where I belong or where I fit in."

The Sweet Valley Sixers is the official sixth-grade newspaper at school. Elizabeth really had spent a lot of time on it last year. I knew she would miss it. I knew, too, that she was missing her best friend, Amy Sutton. Amy and her family moved away over the summer, because Amy's mom had gotten a really great job as a television newscaster in Connecticut. I figured that was probably another reason why Elizabeth was feeling a little at loose ends this year.

"If you've got a lot of extra time this year, why don't you join the drama club?" Maria asked. "It looks like it's going to be a really good group this year. And we're going to put on two musicals."

Maria is also a seventh grader. She has dark eyes, and skin the color of milky coffee, and she's very pretty. She moved to Sweet Valley from Hollywood last year. Believe it or not, she was a child actress, and a successful one, too. She was in movies and TV shows and commercials. Occasionally, you can still see her in reruns or old movies on TV. But as she got older, the parts started slowing down, and her parents wanted to give her a chance at a normal childhood. So they moved here. Maria really likes Sweet Valley. I like it, too, but if I could be in Hollywood, that's where I'd be.

I think about Hollywood all the time. I don't want to be an actress, which is what most people dream about. I want to be a costume designer, because I love clothes—especially clothes that look like costumes.

My family doesn't have much money, so my mom and I have always had to be creative when it comes to clothes. I get most of my clothes from the thrift store. I guess you could say I was the grunge pioneer at Sweet Valley Middle School.

Take today—I had on wide-legged striped pants, a knit cap, and a long vest over a T-shirt. Not to brag or anything, but I do have sort of a flair with clothes. Even Lila Fowler tells me she really likes the way I put things together.

By the way, I have medium-long reddish-brown hair, green eyes, and a few freckles. My nose turns up a little. I hate that, but everybody else says it looks cute.

I took off my black high-tops and rolled up my pants so I could dangle my feet in the water. "Maybe I'll join the drama club this year," I said thoughtfully. "I could work on costumes. What about you, Jessica?"

Jessica smiled and shook her head. "I won't have time. Being president of the Unicorns is a full-time job."

"Hey!" Elizabeth said happily. "I didn't know you were president of the Unicorns this year. That's great, Jess. Congratulations."

"Well," Jessica began, "I'm not president yet. But I will be."

When she explained the dare competition, Elizabeth just shook her head. "Aren't you guys ever going to grow up?" Elizabeth asked.

"What do you mean?" Jessica demanded hotly.

"I mean you're in seventh grade now, Jess. Daring each other to do obnoxious things is dumb."

Jessica tossed her hair back off her shoulders and got to her feet. "You're just saying that because you're not a Unicorn. If you were, you'd understand."

And with that, Jessica got up and stalked angrily into the house.

Two

"It's now or never," Mary Wallace said, giggling. She gave Lila a little push toward the boys' bathroom.

"Cut it out," Lila said, twisting away.

It was just before second period, and all the Unicorns were gathered around the lockers across from the boys' bathroom. Lila had a huge purse slung over her shoulder and I could hear cans of mousse and hair spray clanking around inside it every time she adjusted the strap.

I looked down at my watch. "You've got about two minutes before the first bell."

Lila darted a nervous look at the boys' bathroom, and we all burst into giggles.

Just then, Rick Hunter came around the corner of the lockers, gave us a wave, and then went into the bathroom.

I don't know why, but that just broke us up completely.

Rick is an eighth grader this year and he's really cute. Tall. Dark blond hair. Blue eyes. Always in a good mood.

Mary started making these strange wheezing sounds, and Jessica laughed so hard she began to choke.

Lila's face squinched up. "Ohhhhhhh, I can't go in there. I just can't."

Jessica lifted her fist. "All right! Lila forfeits. That makes me president of the Unicorns."

Lila reached out and pushed Jessica's fist down. "Not so fast, Jessica."

I tapped my watch. "It's zero hour, Fowler."

With that, Lila turned and stalked toward the boys' bathroom. She stiff-armed the door open and disappeared inside.

We all held our breath as though we were waiting for an explosion. "Three . . . two . . . one . . . ," Mary whispered.

Right on cue there were all these outraged howls from inside the boys' bathroom. *"Lila!"* some male voice yelled. *"What are you doing?"*

The next thing we knew, the boys were piling out of there like the place was on fire. Randy Mason, Peter DeHaven, a couple of boys I didn't recognize, and, finally, Rick Hunter came running out.

They looked so funny. You can't believe how red their faces were. Randy Mason always looks a little flustered and nervous. But Peter DeHaven and Rick Hunter are considered "cool guys."

Rick Hunter saw us laughing by the lockers and folded his arms across his chest. "I guess you guys think that's funny, huh?"

We didn't even bother to answer. We just laughed harder.

Rick looked put out and scratched the back of his neck behind his collar. "You know, if a guy had done that—gone into the girls' bathroom, I mean—you wouldn't think it was so funny. You'd think it was a pretty heinous invasion of your privacy."

Mary did her best to look chagrined. But she couldn't keep it up, and she made one of those sputtering motorboat noises.

That totally annoyed Rick. "That's it. No more double standard. Guys need privacy just as much as girls. I'm going to tell Mr. Clark what's going on, and maybe he can explain to Lila why she should do her hair in the *girls'* bathroom."

Wow! Rick was really mad. And actually, I didn't blame him. When I stopped to think about it, Rick was right. If he or Randy or one of the guys had come barging into the girls' bathroom, we *would* think it was horrible.

What had we been thinking? None of us had even considered their feelings for a second.

That's the thing that bothers me sometimes about the Unicorns. I don't know why it is, but sometimes when I'm with them I stop thinking about other people's feelings. Now I was kind of sorry we'd made Lila go into the boys' bathroom.

Still, I wasn't sorry enough to want to get in trouble with Mr. Clark. As school principals go, he's not a complete ogre. In fact, he's a pretty good guy most of the time. But when you're in trouble with Mr. Clark, you're really in trouble. I'm talking notes to parents. Detentions. Suspensions. The works.

Jessica hurried after him and caught his sleeve. "Rick! Wait."

Rick turned around and crossed his arms over his chest. "What?"

Jessica gave him a really nice smile. "We're sorry."

Rick raised one eyebrow as if he didn't believe her.

"We are," she said. "Right, guys?"

We all chimed in, apologizing all over the place. I, for one, was completely sincere. I couldn't tell about the others.

"We won't do it again," Jessica promised. "And we weren't trying to embarrass the boys. It was just part of our dare war. We're trying to pick a president and . . ."

"I get it," Rick said. "OK. OK. I won't go to Mr. Clark if you guys promise to keep your dare war out of the boys' bathroom."

We all promised, and Rick went off to class. Just as he disappeared around the corner, Lila came out of the bathroom with her hair moussed up to the ceiling in a really silly Big Hair style.

I had to hand it to her, she'd really gone the whole nine yards. Jessica led the applause, and we all began laughing again.

"Thank you," Lila said, bowing and curtsying. Then she quickly scanned the hallway. "Are we safe, or did somebody run to get a teacher?"

"You're safe, thanks to Jessica," Ellen said. "She talked Rick Hunter out of complaining to Mr. Clark."

Lila reached out, and she and Jessica high-fived each other in a very comradely way.

I felt better. Dare war or no dare war, it was nice to know the Unicorns looked out for one another.

By fourth period, Lila had combed all the mousse out of her hair. She and Jessica and I were sitting together in science class at the table toward the back of the room where we always sat. The science room has about eight long, high lab tables instead of desks. And instead of chairs, we sit on tall stools.

Mr. Swenson was up at the board, reminding us how to draw a graph.

"Well?" Lila whispered at Jessica.

"Well what?" Jessica whispered back.

"You've only got fifteen more minutes before class is over. Are you going to hide his chalk or not?"

"Of course I am," Jessica whispered.

Across the room, I could see Lois Waller, Caroline Pearce, and Randy Mason all watching us with interested expressions on their faces. It was as if they knew something was going to happen.

After Lila's stunt this morning, word had gotten around the school that the Unicorns were having a dare war. Not to brag or anything, but the Unicorns have a big reputation around school. A dare war to pick a president is pretty big news, so I knew people were talking about it.

"That's it," Mr. Swenson said, putting his chalk down and turning toward the class. "Let me just clarify one or two more points, and then I'll let you talk quietly with your lab partners about your experiments."

Jessica smiled and winked at me. "When we break up into lab groups, I'll make my move."

When the groups were working, Mr. Swenson always liked to go from table to table to see if anybody had any questions. It would be easy for Jessica to get to the front of the room, hide the chalk, and get back to her seat without Mr. Swenson noticing.

I looked up at the big clock on the wall. There wasn't much more time. If Mr. Swenson didn't finish talking soon, there might not be time for the class to break up into groups

He went on and on and on. Usually, I like his class. But now I was too nervous to listen.

I could see that Jessica was getting nervous, too. The minutes were ticking by, and Mr. Swenson was showing no signs of wrapping it up. If Jessica couldn't perform her dare, that meant Lila was president.

Lila's lips were twitching, as if she was trying

hard not to laugh. A few more minutes and she would have it in the bag.

". . . and I think that's all I need to tell you about today," Mr. Swenson was saying.

Jessica let out her breath in a relieved sigh and grinned at me. "All right. Here we go."

Suddenly he snapped his fingers. "Oh!" He glanced at the clock. "Only a few more minutes. Well, I guess that's enough time." He picked up his chalk and began to draw a second graph. "Copy this graph, people. It will help when we break up into small groups tomorrow."

This was *terrible.* The easiest, simplest dare in the whole history of the Unicorn Club, and Jessica was going to blow it.

I couldn't stand it. I had to do something.

I wiggled back and forth on my stool and then . . . *wham!* I accidentally on purpose fell backward and landed on the floor with a big thump.

Everybody in the class jumped to their feet and craned their necks in my direction to see what was going on.

"Mandy! Are you OK?" Jessica gasped.

Mr. Swenson turned quickly and came hurrying back to where I was sprawled on the floor.

"Oh, dear. Oh, dear," he said nervously. "Mandy? Are you all right?"

"I'm OK," I said. "I just sort of . . . my stool was a little wobbly and . . ."

Mr. Swenson peered at the stool through his

glasses. "Hmmmmm," he murmured as he tested the legs of the stool. "Some of these stools are old and a bit unsteady."

Jessica was still hovering over me with a look of concern on her face. I couldn't believe she was being so dense. I caught her eye and jerked my head toward the board.

Her mouth fell open when she realized the whole thing was a setup. But Jessica Wakefield is nothing if not a fast thinker.

While Mr. Swenson and Peter DeHaven grabbed my arms and hauled me to my feet, Jessica zipped up to the front of the room, took the chalk, dropped it in a potted plant, and then got back into her seat just as Mr. Swenson was telling everybody please not to rock on their stools.

A couple of people had noticed Jessica's little trip to the front, and they began to giggle when Mr. Swenson went back to the front of the room.

He reached for the chalk and raised his eyebrows in surprise. "Hmmmmm," he said again in his absentminded-professor way. "Now, what have I done with my chalk?"

Jessica put her hand up in front of her face and smiled at me. "Thanks, Mandy," she whispered.

I smiled back. "What are friends for?"

"OK. We're back at ground zero," Mary said, unwrapping her sandwich. "It's time for round two of the dare war."

All the Unicorns were gathered at the Unicorner, the table in the cafeteria where we always sat. It was so much emptier than it was last year, it was a tiny bit depressing.

Lila's eyes were flashing. She pushed her potato chips away and began to scribble on a piece of paper. "The last dare I gave Jessica was too easy. This time . . ." She shook her head and smiled to let Jessica know she was really in for it.

Jessica grabbed a notebook from Mary and thought for a minute before starting to scribble herself. She finished writing with a big flourish, dramatically ripped the paper out of the notebook, and handed it to Ellen.

Ellen opened both pieces of paper. "Wow!" She got a really nervous look on her face and shoved the papers into Mary's hand. "You read them."

Mary cleared her throat. "Lila hereby officially dares Jessica Wakefield *to paint a purple stripe along the bank of lockers in the South Hall.*"

Everybody gasped.

"And Jessica Wakefield hereby officially dares Lila Fowler *to steal Mrs. Arnette's hairnet and wear it to Casey's ice cream parlor.*"

Whoa!

Everybody had stopped eating, and there was a heavy silence at the table. I had this really bad feeling in my stomach. Like things were getting out of hand. Practical jokes like hiding chalk and going into the wrong bathroom were one thing. Painting lockers and stealing hairnets were another.

I watched Lila and Jessica eyeing each other. I found myself wishing that one of them would back down. If one did, the other one would, too. And if Jessica and Lila both backed out, nobody in the club would blame them for it.

But there was a steely glint in Jessica's eye and a stubborn tilt to Lila's chin.

The heavy feeling in my stomach got heavier as the seconds ticked by.

Ever notice how in a situation like this, there's always a little window of opportunity to get out of it? And if you act quickly enough, you can back down with honor. You can take it back no matter what it is—an insult, a joke, *a dare*.

But if you wait too long, you lose your chance. Then if you back down, or apologize, or say *just kidding*, you look like a chicken.

Tick. Tick. Tick.

Back down, I mentally pleaded with them both. *Back down before it's too late.*

Tick. Tick. Tick.

Bam!

Somebody banged a plate down on the counter and it sounded like a window of opportunity being shut with a bang.

It was too late to back out now. Things had gone too far. I didn't feel good about it, but I didn't know what to do except go along with the club and hope for the best.

Three

"Yuck!" Caroline Pearce complained loudly the next morning in the hallway at school. She held up her hand to reveal a big splotch of purple paint that ran from the heel of her hand up her forearm. "It's wet."

"You're telling me," Randy Mason said angrily. "Look at my sweater." He turned around and showed Lois Waller, Peter DeHaven, Rick Hunter, and a bunch of other people the purple paint on his sweater where he had leaned against the lockers.

All around me, I could hear the angry buzz of students as they arrived at their lockers and discovered the long stripe of wet purple paint that ran all the way down the central bank of lockers.

Jessica had told me last night that she had gone to the paint store and bought a small can of purple paint and that she was planning to get to school super early so she could get the paint into the school, do the stripe, and then hide the incriminating paint can.

Since Jessica hates getting up early, I'd gone to bed feeling pretty secure that she'd oversleep and then give up on the idea.

But as soon as I'd gotten to school, I realized I'd been underestimating her. "How did you manage to get up so early?" I asked when I saw her grinning at me by the lockers.

"I didn't." Jessica giggled. "I just stayed up all night."

Just then, Lila came down the hall with Mary and Ellen. They began giggling when they saw all the confusion.

"It's not funny, Jessica," Randy snapped. "This is my favorite sweater."

Jessica opened her eyes wide and batted her eyelashes. "Gee, Randy," she said in an innocent voice, "I'm sorry about your sweater, but why are you telling *me?*"

The crowd groaned. "Oh, come on, Jessica," somebody said. "Everybody knows the Unicorns are behind this."

Randy shook his head. "I wish you guys would just pick a new president already."

There were several nods of agreement.

"The sooner this dare war is over," Caroline Pearce said, "the safer we'll all be."

Several people were grumbling as they wandered off. Jessica shot me a triumphant look and turned just in time to see . . . *Mr. Clark standing right behind us.*

He looked really mad. "I don't know who is responsible for this act of vandalism," he said in this low voice. "And I am reluctant to make any accusations without concrete proof." He raised one eyebrow and stared at me until I thought I might vaporize. "I have my suspicions, though. And my advice to you girls is to step very carefully. Do I make myself clear?"

"Yes, sir," I said quickly.

"Yes, sir," Jessica piped in.

"Yes, sir," Lila added.

Ellen Riteman is the kind who tends to freeze up in a crisis. She was just standing there staring at Mr. Clark with big, scared eyes. I gave her a little jab with my elbow and she seemed to come around. "Yes, sir," she squeaked.

Mr. Clark stared at us for about another two hours, then he slowly turned and walked back down the hall toward the office.

Beads of sweat were trickling down my neck, and my heart was pounding against my rib cage. "That's it," I said finally. I didn't care what they thought anymore. Lila and Jessica were at war, and we were *all* going to wind up getting in trouble. I was getting kind of mad about it. Mad enough not to just want to go along anymore. "I think it's time to call it quits on the dare war."

"I agree," Mary said. "The Unicorns are supposed to be popular, and we're not making any friends with stunts like this. I say the dare war is off."

"OK by me," Jessica said cheerfully. "Does that mean Lila concedes?"

"No way!" Lila protested. "If Jessica thinks she's going to be president, then the dare war is still on."

Mary shook her head. Ellen looked at the floor. When you got right down to it, there was nothing any of us could do to stop it.

See? This is why we needed a president. If somebody had been in charge, they could have just made the decision that the dare war was off.

Now the whole thing was taking on a life of its own. And I couldn't help wondering where it was going to lead.

I didn't see Jessica, Lila, or anybody else for the rest of the day. And after school, Mrs. Arnette asked me to stay a few minutes after class to talk about my book report on *A Tale of Two Cities*, by Charles Dickens.

I had compared it to starting a new school year. That first line—*"It was the best of times, it was the worst of times"*—seemed to sum up the way I was feeling about everything.

It was the best of times because I was a Unicorn. I had all the teachers I liked. My mom had extended my bedtime an hour. And best of all, I was healthy and I felt good. Last year, I had cancer.

I'm OK now. But let me tell you, there's nothing like having cancer to make you really appreciate your good health. Feeling good is not something I take for granted anymore.

Getting back to the book report, it was the worst of times because, as I said before, I suddenly realized how much about life I didn't know. It seemed that every day I was running into some new word or idea that I'd never heard of before. My body was changing. My feet were, like, *huge.* And I had one permanent pimple. It moved around. But it was always somewhere. If it wasn't on my nose, it was on my chin. And if it wasn't on my chin, it was on my cheek.

Anyway, that was sort of the gist of my book report, and Mrs. Arnette had a lot of nice things to say about the way I had written it and the ideas I had expressed.

People laugh at Mrs. Arnette, but I think she might be my favorite teacher, even if she is kind of old and a fashion disaster. She wears this hairnet over her bun, which looks really uncool. Everybody calls her the Hairnet behind her back.

If I were a little older, I would give her some friendly advice, like *Lose the hairnet.* But I thought it might sound presumptuous coming from a kid— even if the kid is a seventh grader and a Unicorn.

Suddenly, I remembered Lila's dare. She was supposed to steal Mrs. Arnette's hairnet.

When Mrs. Arnette lowered her head to find something in her desk, I took a quick peek at the back of her hair and saw that the net was still on her bun. Come to think of it, that net was *always* on her bun. So how did Jessica think Lila was ever going to steal it?

She couldn't. It was impossible. Jessica must have known that when she wrote the dare.

What a sneaky dare!

I smiled. It looked as though Jessica had won the dare war once and for all. That meant Jessica was now president of the Unicorns. And as I left Mrs. Arnette's classroom, I felt relieved. The dare war was over.

I ran into Mary Wallace on my way out of the school, and she told me the Unicorns were all at Casey's.

Casey's is the ice cream parlor. It's in the Valley Mall, but it has its own entrance on the street. It has old-fashioned tables and chairs, fifty different kinds of ice cream toppings (including Goobers, my personal favorite), and the best jukebox in town. The walls have pictures of old-fashioned people from the 1890s. I love looking at their hats and dresses. The men all have big handlebar mustaches and bowler hats.

Casey's is so neat that even some of the high school kids hang out there sometimes. I don't really like it when they're there, though, because Lila and

Jessica always try to act all sophisticated when high school kids are around.

But they didn't look very sophisticated when Mary and I walked into Casey's. They looked totally silly.

Lila was sitting at the table right in the middle of the place wearing a hairnet over the whole top of her face. Jessica and Ellen were sitting on either side of her, and the three of them were laughing.

I couldn't believe it. I really couldn't.

Neither could Mary. "How did you do it?" she shrieked.

Lila grinned. "Simple. I snuck into the teachers' lounge and . . ."

"You *what!*" Mary yelped.

My jaw dropped. The teachers' lounge is, like, *sacred.* Students are never even allowed to knock on the door. If they're looking for a teacher, they're supposed to ask another teacher to go into the lounge and look for them.

"Tell us what's in there," Ellen breathed. "What's the big secret?"

"Yeah," Mary said, laughing. "What have they got in there? A jukebox?"

"A disco ball?" Jessica added. "A pinball machine?"

That made everybody laugh—even me. And it was about five minutes before we could stop laughing long enough to listen.

Lila tossed her hair off her shoulders as if she

were real tough. "I staked it out," she said, talking out of the side of her mouth like a guy in an old gangster movie. "Waited until I thought the time was right. Then I buzzed in there, found Mrs. Arnette's locker, and swiped the hairnet. She's got about six of them, you know."

We stopped laughing, and there was a long silence as we all digested this bit of information. It explained a lot—like why Mrs. Arnette was never seen without her hairnet.

Then Lila and Jessica began to giggle again, and so did everybody else. Me, too. It was a nervous giggle, though.

Lots of people around us were darting looks in our direction. Some people were laughing at the hairnet on Lila's head, but some of them were frowning and rolling their eyes, as if they thought we were being stupid.

Suddenly, I felt annoyed at Lila. She looked really full of herself. All because she had snuck into the teachers' lounge and stolen a hairnet so she could make fun of Mrs. Arnette. It was pretty mean.

But before I could say anything, Mary Wallace started talking. "Well, I guess we're right back where we started," she said.

"Time for round three of the dare war," Jessica said.

"Time for the mother of all dares," Lila said.

Mary held her spoon up for our attention. "This time, I say the rest of us issue a dare to Jessica and Lila."

Ellen Riteman smiled. "All right! And I know just the dare."

Lila pulled the hairnet off her hair and sat forward with this expectant look on her face. Jessica sat forward, too.

Ellen motioned to everyone to put their head close so nobody sitting around us could hear her. "Caroline Pearce told me that Mr. Clark has a rowing machine in his office, and that in the mornings he changes into workout clothes and works out in his office. When he does, he *takes off his toupee and hangs it on the coatrack just inside the door of his office.*"

Everybody gasped.

"Mr. Clark wears a toupee?"

"No way!"

Ellen smiled. "I say the Unicorn presidency should go to the candidate who can steal it and hang it on the cafeteria door."

"Come on, guys," I protested. "That's awful."

"I know." Ellen chuckled.

That did it. I picked up my knapsack and stood. "OK. You all can do what you want. But I don't want to know about it." Before anybody could say a word, I threaded my way between the tables and hurried out of Casey's, practically knocking Rick Hunter over as he came in the door.

"Hey!" he protested.

"Sorry," I mumbled. But I don't know if he heard me, and I didn't stop to find out. I was too upset.

"Mandy! Mandy, wait up!"

Jessica was hurrying behind me, but I didn't slow down. She ran and caught up with me on the corner. "What's the matter with you?" she asked. "Why are you acting like such a goody-goody?"

"I am *not* acting like a goody-goody," I yelled angrily. I was so upset I was almost in tears. Sometimes Jessica was so thickheaded. "Listen. It might sound crazy to you, but if Mr. Clark wears a toupee, I say that's his business."

Jessica's eyebrows flew up. "Since when?"

"Since now." I turned away quickly, so she wouldn't ask me any more questions. Then I started walking—fast—in the hope that she wouldn't try to follow me.

Sometimes Jessica Wakefield is my favorite person in the whole world. And sometimes I just want to strangle her.

Last year, I had to have chemotherapy to fight my cancer. It worked, but it made my hair fall out. That was pretty horrible, as you can imagine, and I wore a wig. I didn't try to hide it, but I sure wouldn't have wanted anybody to make fun of me. Or try to make me feel embarrassed about wearing it.

"Mandy!" I heard Jessica shout as I crossed the street. Her voice sounded high and thin and far away. "Aren't you going to help me? Do you want Lila to be president of the Unicorns?"

I didn't even bother to turn and answer, because at that point, I didn't see that there was any difference between Jessica and Lila.

They were both being selfish jerks.

Four

That afternoon, I lay on my bed and stared at the ceiling, trying to figure out what made the Unicorns act so thoughtless and mean when they were all together. None of us as individuals were mean. And we weren't mostly very snobby, either.

Mary Wallace was really nice. She liked everybody and could always find something nice to say to people. Even people who were fat and unpopular, like Lois Waller. Mary was the kind of person who would always partner up with the unpopular kids in lab classes when nobody else would.

Jessica had a wonderful side, too. In fact, it had been Jessica who had first been my friend and gotten me into the Unicorn Club.

Lila seemed mean a lot of the time, but she wasn't. Not really. She was just spoiled. Spoiled rotten, according to most people. But when you got right down to it, Lila was an incredibly loyal friend. She could be competitive, but if you really needed her, she was there.

Ellen?

Yeah. I had to admit Ellen could be mean and snobby. But that was because she was a follower. If the rest of us were acting mean and snobby, then Ellen acted mean and snobby. But if the rest of us were to shave our heads and take up yodeling, Ellen would be a bald yodeler.

Which brought me back to my original question: What made the Unicorns act so mean and snobby?

Was it because we were a club?

"Mom?" I asked that night at dinner. "Do you think belonging to a club is bad?"

It was just me and Archie and my mom for dinner. Cecelia had band practice, which was actually kind of a relief. I needed advice but I didn't want a big speech from Saint Cecelia.

Mom stopped spooning out peas and gave me a funny look. "Why do you ask?"

I poked my mashed potatoes with my fork and looked around our little dining room. When we first moved into this house, we didn't have much money because of all my medical expenses.

So Mom and Archie and Cecelia and I had bought some really cheap unpainted furniture and decided to paint it ourselves. The plan was to stencil some leaves and roses over a coat of antique blue paint.

It turned out to be a much bigger job than we realized. Just as we were getting ready to give up, Janet Howell and Jessica had come over to say hi.

As soon as they saw we needed help, they got on the phone and rounded up the rest of the club. By that afternoon, every Unicorn was over at our house tracing and drawing and painting.

Now our dining room was one of the prettiest rooms I had ever seen—and it was all because of the Unicorns.

Whether they were mean and snobby or not, I realized I really loved the Unicorns. And I loved being a member of the club. Did that mean I was mean and snobby?

"Mandy?" Mom prompted.

I dragged my eyes away from the sideboard and saw that Mom and Archie were both staring at me and waiting for me to say something. "I was just, uh, thinking about the Unicorns. Some people think we're, well, not so nice," I finished weakly. "Snobby," I added in a low tone.

"Clubs give people a sense of belonging," Mom said. "There's nothing wrong with that. Everybody likes to feel that they belong. Clubs are also a way of making a big world seem smaller and more manageable."

I gave her a puzzled look.

"A club is sort of like a family," she went on.

"You wouldn't want everybody in the world in your family, would you?"

Archie shook his head.

"Why not?"

Archie shrugged. "Because you don't like them?"

Mom smiled. "No, silly. Because it would be way too confusing to be related to everybody in the whole world. You'd never be able to remember everybody's name. Or their birthday. Or know how many to expect for dinner."

Archie giggled.

"Wouldn't it be pretty overwhelming if every single person in the world showed up on Sunday night for meat loaf?" she asked.

That made me laugh, too. And I could see what my mom was trying to say.

"But my teacher says that some clubs are bad," Archie said. "Clubs that won't let people in for silly reasons. What makes some clubs OK and other clubs not OK?"

My mom sat back in her seat and thought for a long time before she answered. "That's a hard question. And I don't think anybody knows for sure. But I guess a good club is one in which the members bring out the best in one another. And a bad club is one in which they bring out the worst."

A good club is a club in which the members bring out the best in one another. The words were rolling around in my head that night as I tried to fall asleep.

I still felt confused. I still didn't know how to feel about belonging to the Unicorn Club. Because the Unicorns brought out the best *and* the worst in each other.

My being sick last year had brought out the best in the Unicorns. In the beginning, I sure hadn't been anybody's idea of Unicorn material, with my funky clothes and my zero popularity reading. But they'd taken me in. Visited me. Chipped in for a nicer-looking wig than my mom could afford. Helped us fix up our house.

But now this dare war was bringing out the absolute worst in all of us.

I sighed. It was time to have a talk with the rest of the Unicorns. Time to let them know how I felt. A dare war was a stupid way to elect a president.

Would we elect a class president because he or she was willing to play a mean practical joke?

No.

Would we elect a United States president because he or she was willing to go into the wrong bathroom?

No.

So why were we electing the president of the most important and prestigious girls' club in Sweet Valley that way? It didn't make any sense.

First thing tomorrow morning, I was going to

tell the Unicorns my incredibly insightful thoughts on the subject.

The next morning was really busy. There was an assembly after second period, and I had a history test during fifth period. I absolutely had to get to class on time so I could glance over my notes on the Industrial Revolution and think of five things it had in common with the Technological Revolution. So my incredibly insightful thoughts had to wait till lunch.

I didn't even *see* any other Unicorns until lunchtime. I was on my way to the cafeteria when I heard this big roar of laughter. There was a group of kids standing outside the cafeteria door. And when I got closer, I saw what was causing the commotion.

Hanging from the doorknob was a forlorn-looking furry object. My heart sank.

That's right. You guessed it.

A toupee.

Jessica and Lila were whooping and dancing around it like a couple of Apaches, and making jokes about scalping the principal.

"They did it," Ellen shouted gleefully. "They got into Mr. Clark's office and snatched it. But they had to do it together, so I guess the dare war still isn't over."

Lila and Jessica high-fived each other.

I looked away. I didn't think it was funny at all anymore.

Elizabeth and Maria went by us on their way

into the cafeteria and they didn't even smile. Maria just shook her head, and Elizabeth looked unhappy and sort of embarrassed by the whole thing.

I didn't blame her. I was embarrassed, too. Embarrassed to be a member of the club. I was just opening my mouth to tell them so when I heard this horrible sound.

It was the sound of a throat being cleared.

Everybody heard it at the same time. One by one, every face registered shock—and then fear. Ellen's face went white and Mary's eyes got huge.

Slowly, painfully, we all turned and saw something I'd never expected to see in my whole life.

Mr. Clark—*bald!*

It was so embarrassing, I didn't know where to look. It wasn't that he looked bad or anything. As a matter of fact, he looked better. But Mr. Clark didn't look as if he was in the mood for any fashion advice.

He didn't say anything for a long, long time.

The silence went on and on, and I swear I could hear every heart pounding. Mr. Clark looked from face to face. When he looked at me, I couldn't meet his eyes. I looked down at my feet, which, by the way, looked about ten feet long.

"My office," he said finally. "Now!"

Then he turned and strode away.

We all hesitated a minute. Then Lila and Jessica fell into step behind him. Mary yanked my sleeve and pulled me along with her. And Ellen brought up the rear—carrying Mr. Clark's toupee.

"I'm so surprised and disappointed, I just can't think of what to say," Mom told me when I got home from school that afternoon.

I'd brought home a note from Mr. Clark. All the Unicorns had.

"After the talk we had last night, I can't imagine what made you take part in such a mean-spirited, thoughtless prank."

It was no use saying I hadn't actually taken part in it. I'd known what was going on and hadn't voiced any serious objections. In a way, that made me as responsible as Lila and Jessica.

Mom scanned the note again. "Mr. Clark wants to see all the parents in his office tomorrow after school." She gave me a long look. "Mandy, I don't think I need to explain to you what you've done wrong here, do I?"

I hung my head and shook it.

"Then there's very little I can say to you that you don't already know. I think you should go to your room now and think of a suitable apology to Mr. Clark."

If you've got a mom like mine, then you know how it is. The less they yell, the worse you feel. It would have been easier if she'd screamed at me. As it was, I just felt like the lowest form of life on the planet. At best, something down a few rungs from algae.

I was on my way upstairs when the phone rang.

It was Jessica, and she was speaking in a whisper because she wasn't supposed to be on the phone. She told me her parents were furious and that she was grounded. And that Lila's father was in New York, but the school had called him at his New York office and he was flying back tonight in order to be at the meeting in Mr. Clark's office tomorrow.

This thing was shaping up to be serious.

Serious turned out to be an understatement.

The Unicorns were in big trouble. That was obvious from the minute my mom and I got to the principal's office. Mrs. Knight in the outer office told us to go on into Mr. Clark's office and "join the others." Mr. Clark would be in shortly. She looked really grim.

It was crowded in there when we walked in. Everybody was already there with their parents. I glanced over at Mr. and Mrs. Wakefield. It was the first time I'd ever seen them so angry that they didn't even smile at me. They just sort of bobbed their heads in our direction. My mom bobbed her head at them, and then I felt her hand on my back, pushing me toward two empty chairs next to Mr. Fowler. Mr. Fowler shook hands with my mom and introduced himself.

Mr. Clark walked in a few seconds later. I noticed the toupee was gone.

"Thank you all for coming," he said briskly.

"Each of you received a note outlining the events of yesterday afternoon. Any questions?"

The parents all looked at one another and then shook their heads.

"No," some of them said, or "I don't think so."

"Fine," Mr. Clark said. He sat down on the edge of his desk and crossed his arms across his chest. "I would be well within my rights to suspend each of the girls for a week or more."

Several parents gasped, and Mr. Clark held up his hand. "I'm not going to do that. Not yet, anyway. What I *am* going to do is insist that the girls perform thirty hours of service for the Sweet Valley Community Services Organization."

"Is that thirty hours per person or thirty hours collectively?" Lila asked.

"Lila!" Mr. Fowler said sharply.

"Thirty hours per person," Mr. Clark answered.

Lila rolled her eyes, and Mr. Fowler gave my mom an embarrassed look as if to say *What am I going to do with her?*

Most of the other parents, including my mom, nodded approvingly.

"That's a wonderful organization," Mrs. Wakefield said. "I've done a lot of fund-raising on their behalf."

"I'm not familiar with it," Mr. Riteman said.

"It's a resource center for people who are in need," Mrs. Wakefield explained. "They provide a range of services. They have several legal and social workers on staff. One of the most important things they do, though, is operate the Sweet Valley Child Care Center for low-income parents."

"I'm glad you mentioned the Child Care Center," Mr. Clark said to Mrs. Wakefield. "Because that's where they desperately need more hands. I thought the girls could help out there after school."

"I think that's a well-thought-out and reasonable punishment," Mrs. Wallace said. "It won't hurt any of these girls to perform a little community service." She stood up and picked up her purse. "So if that's all, I'll be on my way."

Mrs. Wallace is one of those people who's always running late and trying to hurry things along so she can get to her next appointment.

"That's not all," Mr. Clark said ominously.

Mrs. Wallace froze and sat back down.

"The Unicorns will, of course, have to pay for my property." (I noticed he didn't say toupee.) "It was soiled and torn in all the excitement. It will have to be replaced. And last, as of today the Unicorn Club is on probation," Mr. Clark said. "If they do one more rotten thing, the club will be forcibly abolished."

That got a reaction.

"Probation!" Jessica squeaked.

"No way," Ellen protested.

Even some of the parents murmured under their breath.

"Don't you think that's a little severe?" Mrs. Riteman said in a faint voice.

"I don't think so at all," Mr. Clark said, glowering. "I've had a lot of complaints about the Unicorns recently from students as well as teachers. If they step out of line one more time, I'm going to exercise my authority to ban any association or club that, in my opinion, is counterproductive to the efficiency and morale of the school."

Complaints from teachers? Counterproductive to the efficiency and morale of the school?

We were supposed to be the most popular girls at school. The prettiest. The girls that everybody wanted to be like.

Now here was Mr. Clark talking about us as if we were some kind of pest infestation.

And he was right. The Unicorns had gotten carried away with pranks and dares and tricks. Maybe probation was a good thing if it would make everybody think twice about stuff like that from now on.

As we all shuffled across the parking lot of the school, I looked at my friends, and I hoped they were feeling the same way. As mad as I'd been at the Unicorns yesterday, I really didn't want the club to be disbanded.

What I wanted was for us to be the kind of club that I could be proud to say I belonged to.

Five

"Maybe this isn't going to be so bad," Mary said the next Monday afternoon. "Elizabeth volunteers at the Child Care Center, and she told me she likes it a lot."

Jessica made a face. "Yeah. But that's because Elizabeth is the kind of person who likes changing dirty diapers and things like that."

"Diapers!" Lila gasped. "Yuck! Are all the kids in diapers?"

"No," Jessica said. "According to Elizabeth, most of the kids are older than that. But some of them are still in diapers. And sometimes people leave little babies at the Center."

"I like babies," Mary said happily. "I think they're fun."

"Good, then we'll put you in charge of diapers," Jessica said, giggling.

We were on our way to the Sweet Valley Child Care Center to start working off our sentence. The Center was about ten blocks from school. Elizabeth Wakefield and some of the other kids from school volunteered there pretty often, but I'd never seen the inside of it. None of the Unicorns had.

When we turned the last corner and saw the place, my heart sank. It didn't look too promising.

Because the Center is a nonprofit organization and funded by grants and donations, the building isn't very fancy. In fact, it's downright ugly—a low, squat, L-shaped brick building at the end of a dead-end street. There was nothing else around it, no shops or houses or anything. It just sat there by itself, surrounded by a big sea of vacant lot. In the side yard, there were some swings and a sandbox. But most of the yard needed mowing, and there were a lot of weeds growing along the sagging chain-link fence at the far end of the property.

"This place is, like, totally depressing," Lila said as we made our way up the front walk toward the double glass doors of the entrance.

"Maybe it won't be so bad when we get inside," Mary said brightly.

The inside was even worse. All faded linoleum and ugly acoustical tiles.

The place was run by this lady called Mrs. Willard, who wasn't exactly the friendliest person I've ever met.

When we introduced ourselves, she never even smiled. She looked us over like we were convict labor. Mr. Clark must have filled her in on why we were there.

"I feel like we're a chain gang," Mary said out loud, almost as if she were reading my mind.

It was true. Mrs. Willard did treat us like a chain gang. A bunch of criminals that she was going to have to watch every minute to make sure we didn't escape or rob the place. Under the circumstances, I was amazed that she was even going to let us look after the kids.

After giving us a long lecture about what a big and important responsibility it was to help look after the children of the community, she crooked her finger and told us to follow her.

We fell into step, single-file, and followed her down the hall past some offices. Inside the offices, I saw a few people working at desks and gathered around tables piled with papers. Mrs. Willard waved a hand in their direction. "There are several volunteers and employees who help out here," she said, "but over the next two weeks we're going to be especially shorthanded. Two of our staff members are on vacation, and some of our volunteers who usually work with the children are working hard in the afternoons on our grant proposal for next year's funding. This is why we need you girls here every afternoon. And we need all five of you. In order to maintain the legal ratio of adults to children, we need all five of you every afternoon."

I heard several heavy sighs from my fellow Unicorns.

"The main playroom is in here," she announced as we turned a corner. Then she opened a set of swinging double doors and . . . whooosh!

The noise almost knocked me over.

There were kids *everywhere*. Kids yelling. Kids shoving. Kids screaming. Kids crying.

It was pandemonium.

Two little girls in the corner were pounding on each other, fighting over a toy. A little boy took one look at us, and then threw up on the floor. And suddenly, from out of nowhere, another incredibly foul odor began floating through the room. Somebody had had an accident.

I looked at Mary to see if she was getting into that diaper frame of mind. But she just wrinkled her nose and looked as overwhelmed as I felt.

Mrs. Willard didn't seem the least bit fazed. "As you can see, we desperately need more volunteers, so you girls have your work cut out for you."

For the next half hour, she showed us where they kept the cleaning supplies, the first-aid equipment, the snack supplies, the plastic cups, and the plastic plates.

Then she bugged out and we were on our own.

Lila shook her head. "This is just not me," she shouted over the noise.

"It's not any of us," Mary exclaimed as she tried

to separate the two girls who were still fighting over the toy. I immediately went to her aid.

"Yeah, but I'm getting out of this," Lila sniffed. "Come on, Mandy. I may need you to tell my dad I'm not exaggerating."

There was a pay phone in the hall, and I went out with her to make the call. Unfortunately, there was already somebody on the phone. A lady with short blond hair wearing a faded-looking business suit.

"No," I heard her saying, "I don't have exactly that kind of experience. No, I don't have a college degree, but I . . . What? . . . I would work very hard. . . . I . . . I . . . Yes. . . . I understand but . . ."

She glanced at me and Lila. She looked incredibly unhappy. "Can't I even come in for an interview?" she pleaded. She listened for a long time. "Thank you anyway," she said finally. She hung up and gave us a rueful smile. "Sorry to keep you waiting."

"That's OK," I said, trying to give her an encouraging smile. "Are you trying to find a job?"

She nodded. "It's not easy. There are fewer and fewer jobs every day. But I do have two job interviews this afternoon," she added cheerfully.

"My mom had a hard time finding a job too," I said. "It took her a long time."

The lady gave us both a big smile and held out her hand. "I'm Linda McMillan. Are you girls volunteers?"

"Uh, sort of." I wasn't sure whether being sentenced to work here counted as volunteering or not.

"I can't tell you what a wonderful place this is. If I couldn't leave Ellie here while I went out to look for work, I don't know what I'd do."

A wonderful place? Hmmmm . . . I guess maybe from her point of view it was.

That's when I noticed the little girl who had been hiding behind her skirt. She was tiny, with long dark curls and big brown eyes. So that was Ellie?

"Hi," I said with a smile.

But Ellie was too busy looking at Lila to answer.

Mrs. McMillan looked at her watch. "I've got to go. Can I leave Ellie with you girls?" She reached down and detached each one of Ellie's little fingers from the hem of her skirt.

"Sure," I said. "And good luck," I added as she hurried down the hall.

The whole time we had been talking, Lila had just stood there looking bored and distant, as if she really wasn't interested in the Center or Mrs. McMillan's problems.

I held my hand out to Ellie. But Ellie ignored it and went straight for Lila, reaching to grab the hem of her suede skirt and looking happily up at her.

Lila glanced briefly down, then she stepped up to the phone and dropped in a quarter. She dialed the number of her dad's office and had to go through a couple of secretaries before she got him.

As soon as he got on the phone, Lila began talking in this pouty, little-girl voice. "Dadddyyyyy, this place is horrible. It's full of little kids. And Daddy"—she turned her back and lowered her voice—"it *smells*."

I could hear Mr. Fowler's voice on the other end of the line.

Lila shrugged. "Diapers, I guess. . . . Yes, I know that's what dirty diapers smell like. But I don't see why . . . Well, what I was thinking is that maybe we could hire somebody to take my place. Maybe somebody from your office. You said most of them didn't have enough to do."

I could hear Mr. Fowler shouting now.

"I would pay for it myself, out of my allowance."

He shouted even louder, and then . . . *click.*

Lila's jaw dropped in indignation as she replaced the receiver. "He said *no* and hung up. Can you believe it? Have you ever heard of anything so unreasonable in your life? Even after I said I'd pay for a replacement myself."

I shrugged. "I guess he wants you to learn a lesson."

"I'll teach him a lesson," she said through gritted teeth. She started searching through her bag for another quarter. "I'm going to call again and cry. That'll get me out of this."

While Lila was still rooting angrily through her bag, Ellie reached up and began tugging at her elbow.

"Not now," Lila snapped.

Ellie kept tugging.

"What?"

Ellie motioned for Lila to bend down.

Lila rolled her eyes, as if she was really annoyed, and bent down. "What?"

"You're pretty," Ellie whispered in a little shy voice.

Lila's eyebrows shot up to her hairline and her mouth popped open again. "Oh," she said in a soft, surprised tone.

Ellie gave her a sweet and adoring smile.

"Oh," Lila said again. She was really pleased, I could tell. "Thank you."

Ellie smiled again and then turned and ran toward the playroom.

Lila watched her go with this funny expression on her face. Then she noticed me looking at her, and her face clouded over again. She stood up and tossed her hair back. "Oh, well," she said in a resigned tone. "One hour down. Twenty-nine more to go."

I didn't hear anything more about her calling her dad again after that.

Six

Elizabeth Wakefield came by about half an hour after we arrived to help us out. She was an old hand at this, and I couldn't help admiring the way she got all the kids calmed down and settled into some kind of activity almost immediately.

She sat one little boy on the floor with finger paints. She got some of the girls involved in a game of musical chairs, and she got another of the little boys busy putting together a puzzle while one of the toddlers sat beside him with a picture book.

"Thank goodness Elizabeth is here," Jessica said. She and I had gone over to the kitchen area, because Mrs. Willard had asked us to give the kids their afternoon snacks. The kitchen was at the far end of the playroom and had lots of cupboards, a sink, and a refrigerator behind a long white Formica counter.

"Bet you fifty cents I can get her to do my work for me," Jessica added with a cocky grin.

"How are you going to do that?"

"You know those book reports we just did for the Hairnet's class?"

"Yeah. I did mine on *A Tale of Two Cities*."

"I did mine on *Tom Sawyer*."

"I've read that," I said.

"Two words," she said, holding up two fingers. A sneaky smile was forming on her face. "Picket fence."

I knew exactly what she was talking about, and I started to giggle. If you've ever read *Tom Sawyer*, you probably know what Jessica was trying to do. In the book, Tom, who's the main character, is told to paint a fence. He doesn't want to, so he decides to get his friends to do all the work by pretending that painting the fence is loads of fun and a big honor. When his friends ask if they can paint some, he acts really reluctant. The more reluctant he is to let them paint, the more determined to paint they become. By the end of the chapter, Tom is kicking back, watching all his friends paint the fence.

I giggled as I watched Elizabeth walk over to the kitchen area. She opened the cabinet over the sink, but before she could reach up and get down the plastic plates, Jessica beat her to it. "Better let me," Jessica said. "Ms. Willard told me the snacks were my responsibility."

Elizabeth looked a little surprised. "Sure, Jess. I'll just get the milk and . . ."

Jessica whirled around and opened the refrigerator. "I'll get the milk," she said quickly. She reached in and took out the carton. "I wouldn't want it to get spilled."

Elizabeth opened her eyes wide. "Are you saying I might spill the milk?" she demanded.

"Of course not," Jessica said soothingly. Then she gently moved Elizabeth to the side, as if she were in the way. "Excuse me," she said, reaching into the cabinet for napkins.

Elizabeth opened a box of graham crackers and Jessica gave her a patronizing smile. "Maybe I'd better do that," Jessica said, firmly taking the box from Elizabeth's hand. "Mrs. Willard was very specific about how this was supposed to be done, and I want to be sure we do it right."

Elizabeth's mouth fell open. Then she snatched the box of graham crackers from Jessica's hand and began angrily counting them out onto the plates. "I've been volunteering here since last year," she said hotly, "and . . ."

A little smile was playing around the corner of Jessica's mouth as she watched Elizabeth put the graham crackers on the plates. Elizabeth must have noticed it, too.

". . . and I've never seen anyone do as good a job as you're doing," she finished, shoving the box of graham crackers back into Jessica's hands.

Jessica's face fell, and I couldn't help laughing out loud. Elizabeth Wakefield is no dummy. A little smile was playing around her mouth now.

"In fact," she went on, "you guys are doing such a good job, I don't think you need any help at all."

"Elizabeth!" Jessica wailed.

"This is great, Jess." Elizabeth grinned broadly. "Now that the Unicorns are here, I can take a vacation for a while."

"*Elizabeth!*" Jessica and I both wailed together.

But Elizabeth just waved. "Have fun," she said, laughing and fluttering her fingers. Then she scooted around the counter and across the playroom and disappeared through the double doors.

We just stood there miserably, watching her go.

"Hey!" An indignant little voice interrupted the silence. "You didn't give everybody the same number of graham crackers."

Jessica and I both looked up and saw this cute little face peering at us over the counter.

"Man. You guys are doing it all wrong."

Jessica's face clouded over. "Tough," she said. Then she frowned. "Don't you have something to do?"

"It's story time," he said. "You're supposed to read us a story."

"Well, I can only do one thing at a time," Jessica responded in this really cranky tone. "Do you want a story or do you want a snack?"

He cocked his head. "Elizabeth gives us snacks *and* tells us a story."

"I'm not Elizabeth," Jessica snapped.

"No kidding," he snapped back.

Jessica shook her head. "This place is gross."

Half an hour later, I was ready to agree.

Ever notice how one or two kids are sweet? But if you get a whole bunch of them in one place they turn into a noisy, smelly, burpy mob?

The kids were all blurring together, and I kept losing count. But it looked to me as though there were two toddlers, a baby, and Ellie, and then there was the group that Mary nicknamed the Wild Bunch.

The Wild Bunch was made up of Arthur Foo; Sandy and Allison Meyer, the two little girls who were always fighting; and a little girl named Yuky (pronounced "Yoooky," but the other members of the Wild Bunch called her "Yucky," as in brussels-sprouts yucky), who seemed to be in constant motion but never said a word. And the ringleader, Oliver, the little boy who had been so critical of Jessica. Turns out he had been at the Center for the longest time. He knew everybody and everything, and he didn't mind speaking up if he thought something wasn't being done right.

The only two people in the room who seemed to be having no problems at all were Ellie and Lila. Lila sat in a rocker in the corner with Ellie on her lap, and the two of them spent the whole afternoon happily admiring each other. I'd never seen anything like it.

"Hey!" I heard Jessica shout about ten minutes before we were supposed to leave. "Cut that out."

I looked over just in time to see Oliver happily cutting up one of the picture books with a pair of grown-up scissors—definitely contraband.

"I am cutting it out," Oliver joked. And he held up the scissors and snipped them in the air to illustrate his joke.

"Give me those," Jessica demanded, starting toward him with her hand out.

"No way," Oliver argued.

Jessica dove forward and successfully grabbed the scissors. Oliver jerked away, lost his balance, and fell back onto one of the toddlers.

The toddler let out one long shrill squeal, and it was like the signal they had all been waiting for. The next thing I knew, the room had erupted into a full-scale riot.

Sandy and Allison teamed up and began chasing Arthur Foo around the crafts table, while one of the toddlers—the one in the playpen—squealed encouragement.

Mary, who was standing behind the kitchenette counter spreading peanut butter on some crackers, began to laugh. "Bloodthirsty little thing, isn't she— *Hey!*" she yelled as Arthur ran by and swiped the peanut butter jar. *"Put that down!"*

Arthur jammed his fist down into the jar and then turned and pelted Sandy and Allison with handfuls of peanut butter. Both of them came to a halt, let out a scream, and then took off running in the opposite direction.

"Come back here!" Mary screamed at Arthur.

Splat!

A great big gob of peanut butter came hurtling across the counter and landed right on the shoulder of Mary's favorite purple angora sweater.

Mary let out an outraged shriek, then she vaulted over the counter in one swift movement and headed toward him.

Arthur veered around the puzzle table and headed for the musical chairs.

Mary cut diagonally across the room, jumped over the chairs, and headed him off by the building blocks. She scooped him up under the arm, and he began kicking.

"Stop that!" Mary ordered, holding him away from her body.

Arthur just screamed louder and kicked harder.

Meanwhile, Jessica was chasing Oliver around and around and around the table. Allison and Sandy had given up on Arthur and turned their attention toward Yuky.

Ellen was hurrying to the rescue when she stepped in a glob of peanut butter, went skidding across the floor and . . .

Crash!

She slid right into the finger paints and kept going—leaving red, green, blue, and yellow skid marks behind her before she plowed into the musical chairs and knocked them over like bowling pins.

Lila and Ellie were just diving for cover when the door flew open.

"What is the meaning of this?" shouted an outraged voice.

Everybody in the room froze.

I lifted my head and felt my heart stop.

Mrs. Willard was standing there with two people who looked like parents and two women from the office.

Nobody said a word. Even the kids were dead silent. There wasn't one sound except for the steady drip of milk as it rolled off the edge of the counter and hit the floor.

"Maintaining order among the children is the most important part of the job. If you can't even maintain order, how do you expect to challenge their intellects? Nurture their emotions? Build their self-esteem?"

Nobody answered.

We were standing in a line—just like soldiers—while Mrs. Willard paced back and forth yelling at us.

"Girls. I think you know by now that your principal and your parents are serious about this community service. I think you'd better start taking it seriously, too. I'll see you tomorrow."

Nobody said a word as we walked down the hall.

"Hey, Jessica!" a little voice called out.

Jessica turned just in time to see Oliver poke his

head around the corner and stick out his tongue.

"Ohhhh," Jessica groaned. "That kid is such a pain!"

Mary just shook her head. "Anybody else getting the feeling this is going to be the longest two weeks of our lives?"

Seven

The next day I had to stay a few minutes after school to ask Mr. Swenson some questions about the homework assignment, so I didn't walk to the Child Care Center with everybody. Lila had to stay a few minutes late, too, to get a book from the library, so the two of us wound up walking over together.

We'd only gotten a couple of blocks from school when we heard a horn honk. A shabby old car pulled up next to the curb, and I felt Lila's hand on my arm. "Who's that?" she asked in a tense voice. "I don't know anybody who has a car that looks like that."

Neither did I, and it made me a little nervous until I realized it was Mrs. McMillan behind the wheel and Ellie in the passenger seat.

"Hi, girls," she called. "Are you on your way to the Center?"

As soon as Ellie saw Lila, her little face just lit up and she began waving.

Lila smiled and waved back.

"Hop in and I'll drive you," Mrs. McMillan offered.

"Thanks," we both said as we climbed into the backseat. I could see Lila looking around the car with this strange expression on her face. Lila spends most of her time being driven around in a Rolls Royce. I guess being in an old shabby car was a new experience for her.

"It's a beautiful day," Mrs. McMillan said with a smile. "Ellie and I spent all morning in the park today. I'm trying to spend as much time with her as possible before I start work."

"That's great," I said. "Does that mean you got a job?"

"No. But I'm sure I'll get one soon. I have to," she added in a different voice. A more serious voice. "If I don't . . ." Mrs. McMillan trailed off. I could see her face in the rearview mirror, and it looked unhappy.

Ellie twisted in her seat and danced a beat-up–looking doll in a baby dress along the back of the seat. "My new doll," she announced, smiling shyly as she turned it this way and that so we could see it.

"What's her name?" I asked.

Ellie's dimples appeared. "Lila," she whispered.

Lila burst into delighted laughter.

"Her birthday was last week, and that was her present," Mrs. McMillan explained. She smiled. "Of course, it's not really a new doll," she added in a low voice. "It's just new for Ellie. I got it at the thrift store. Until I get a job, that's all I can afford."

"It looks like a great doll," I said in a bright voice.

"Yeah," Lila whispered. But her face had this funny look on it.

A few moments later, we pulled up in front of the Center. Mary was just coming along the sidewalk and waved at us as we climbed out of the back.

I introduced her to Mrs. McMillan while Lila opened Ellie's door and unbuckled her seat belt. "Come on, Ellie," she cooed sweetly. "Let's go inside."

Mrs. McMillan waved and drove off. We stood outside and stared at the building, Lila holding Ellie.

"Think today is going to be better than yesterday?" Mary asked gloomily.

Lila hitched Ellie up on her hip.

I sighed. "It couldn't be worse."

"How's it going?" I asked Jessica when I got inside.

Jessica shook her head. "You just missed it. Mrs. Willard came in and told us if we didn't get our act together today she's going to tell Mr. Clark."

"Oh boy," I breathed.

"I hate this place," Jessica grumbled. "I don't

think I'm going to be able to stand twenty-seven more hours of this."

Just then, a terrible odor came drifting toward us. I wrinkled my nose, and so did Jessica. "*Mary!*" we both called out. "*Diaper duty!*"

The rest of the afternoon, we had what you might call an armed truce broken by minor skirmishes.

Arthur Foo, the little boy who had thrown the peanut butter, was in good form. Turned out, throwing anything goopy and sticky was his favorite sport. Twice, he lobbed big handfuls of finger paint at other kids.

Fortunately, finger paint is water-based.

Mary took him over and gave him a Nerf ball to throw. At first, he wasn't too interested. But after Mary set up a target for him—other than herself, which was his first choice—he spent the rest of the afternoon harmlessly occupied.

Allison and Sandy Meyer were at it again. As you may have already figured, if they weren't fighting with each other, they were ganging up on somebody else. They had to be watched every minute, and Ellen sort of made them her responsibility.

We had two toddlers again that afternoon, and I kept an eye on them. They were both in the playpen and I was playing tug-a-rattle with one through the bars when I felt something at my elbow. I looked down and saw Yuky peering at me.

"Hi," I said with a smile. "My name is Mandy."

Yuky gave me a shy little smile, then she took off and hid under the table. I could feel her watching me all afternoon. And every once in a while, I would make another effort to talk to her. But Yuky still wasn't talking.

Lila and Ellie were inseparable. They spent the next hour making up a story about a princess. I had a feeling Lila was filling in a few details from real life.

They looked so happy sitting there, I almost felt jealous. None of us could do anything right, and Lila Fowler, of all people, could do no wrong.

"Give me all your fours," Jessica demanded.

"Go fish," Oliver crowed.

Jessica rolled her eyes and picked a card off the pile.

She and Oliver and I were sitting around the little round table playing cards.

"Hey!" she cried sharply. She reached across the table and grabbed Oliver's arm.

"Hey yourself!" Oliver yelped. "What do you think you're doing?"

But Jessica just ignored him, reached up into his sleeve, and pulled out a playing card. She looked at it, scowled, then held it up for me to see. "It's a four. You said you didn't have any fours. This is cheating, Oliver."

"So?"

"So, nobody likes a cheater," Jessica snapped.

With that, Oliver reached over and plunged his little fist into the pocket of Jessica's jacket. "Oh yeah?" he asked, pulling up a pair of cards. "Who are you calling a cheater, cheater?"

Jessica's face turned a deep red. She narrowed her eyes at Oliver, and he narrowed his eyes back.

"I'll bet nobody likes you at all," he said in a sassy tone.

Jessica slammed her cards down, stood up, and tossed her hair off her shoulders. "It's snack time," she announced haughtily.

Oliver jumped up to follow her to the kitchen area.

"And if you try to tell me how many graham crackers to put on each plate, I'll wring your little neck," she added with a sour expression.

"That kid is driving me crazy," Jessica grumbled as she put the plastic cups out on the counter.

I got the milk out of the refrigerator and started pouring.

"He follows me around," Jessica continued. "He talks back. And he contradicts every single thing I say."

"Gee," I said. "Now you know what it's like to have a little brother."

It was funny, but watching Jessica and Oliver together really was like watching a brother and sister. They bickered constantly and were constantly putting each other down.

"We're short one glass," I said as I poured the milk into plastic cups.

"Here's another one," Jessica said. She picked one up out of the sink, rinsed it out, and put it on the counter.

"No! No! No!"

We both whirled around and saw Mrs. Willard watching us and shaking her head in a disapproving way. She picked up the glass that Jessica had put on the counter and put it back in the sink.

"I explained the procedures for hygiene. There's no excuse for this kind of sloppiness. Glasses must be washed before reuse. Day-care centers fight a constant battle with colds and viruses. Our best defense is rigid hygiene."

"I rinsed it with hot water," Jessica argued.

"Rinsing is not washing," Mrs. Willard said.

Jessica sighed impatiently. "We needed a glass and—"

"I don't want to listen to excuses," Mrs. Willard interrupted. "I want you to do it right."

"Why don't you use paper cups if you're that worried about germs?" Jessica demanded in a rude voice.

"Reusable cups are both more economical and ecologically sound," Mrs. Willard snapped.

"Well, if I were running this Center—"

"You are not," Mrs. Willard said curtly. "A fact for which the children should be heartily grateful." She handed Jessica the glass. "Now wash this glass with soap and hot water."

As Mrs. Willard stalked out, there was dead silence in the room.

Jessica turned toward the sink, grabbed a sponge and some soap, and got to work on the glass, grumbling and muttering the whole time. Her voice got louder and louder as she scrubbed.

"I hate being here," she said angrily. "I hate the way it looks. I hate the way it smells. I hate being surrounded by all these little kids."

A couple of the kids stopped what they were doing and looked over in Jessica's direction.

"Jessica," Mary said, realizing, as I did, that Jessica's harsh words were being heard all over the playroom.

"They're monsters!" she yelled.

"Jessica!" I hissed. "Be quiet, would you?"

But Jessica was too busy talking, and washing, and banging things around to pay attention. I hurried over to where she was standing to shut her up.

"They're snotty-nosed little rats and I can't wait for my sentence to be up so I can leave here and *never come back.*"

"Jessica!" Lila finally shouted.

"What?" She turned away from the sink and so did I. And that's when she saw that every single kid was watching her and listening to every horrible thing she had said about them.

It was awful. Absolutely awful. You never saw so many hurt faces in your life. Even the really tiny ones looked stricken and unhappy.

And the one who looked the most hurt was Oliver. He wouldn't even look at Jessica. He just turned and ran behind the musical chairs, where he grabbed Peppermint, the big orange cat that lived at the Center, and buried his face in her fur.

I looked at Mary, and she dropped her eyes to the floor. So did Ellen and Lila. So did I. I think we were all feeling the same thing.

Sure, the kids had been bratty and disobedient. But they were just little kids. Jessica didn't need to say such awful things about them.

Then, suddenly—miracle of miracles—a uniformed deliveryman appeared in the doorway with this huge sack. "I have a delivery here from Lowen's toy store."

At the words "toy store," every kid's eyes turned toward the door.

The man looked at his list and began reading. "I've got packages for the following people: Ellie McMillan, Arthur Foo, Sandy Meyer, Allison Meyer, Yuky Park, Oliver Johnson—"

"I'll sign," Lila interrupted, hurrying over and grabbing his clipboard.

He nodded and dropped his boxes.

The kids still didn't quite get it, not even when Lila began handing out the packages.

But as soon as the first box was opened, they got it. They got it big-time. You've never heard so many squeals and giggles in your life. It was better than Christmas. It was like magic.

"Lila," I said, feeling on the verge of tears. "Sometimes you really surprise me."

But Lila didn't say anything, she just kept handing out packages like she was Santa Claus.

A few minutes later, I saw Jessica pick up her backpack and slip quietly out the door.

I knew I should go after her. Try to talk to her about what had happened. As I said before, Jessica isn't a mean person at heart. And I felt pretty sure that she was feeling bad about what she'd done.

I kind of hoped she was. Because I hoped that maybe next time she would think about other people's feelings before she opened her big mouth.

Eight

"Don't tell me," I teased Lila as the two of us walked home from the Center that evening. "The presents were all part of your master plan to change our image at the Center." I was laughing, but it was partly serious. I hadn't exactly felt very proud to be a Unicorn there. And I was grateful to Lila for boosting our popularity rating so high—with the kids, at least.

Lila gave me a thin smile and shook her head. "No. I just wanted to do something for Ellie. Seeing that old doll made me feel sad. See, when I was little, I got zillions of toys on my birthday. New toys. Toys that belonged only to me. I wanted to get Ellie a birthday present. Something new that would belong only to her. And then I realized I couldn't get her a present without getting them all presents. So when I went into the Center this afternoon, I called the toy store, gave them the names and ages of the kids, and told them to put a rush on it."

As I said before, Lila Fowler is spoiled and used to getting her way. But there's no denying that she can be generous. And getting something for every kid showed a lot of sensitivity on her part.

Lila sighed. "I'm learning something, though. You can't fix everything with a present. When Mrs. McMillan came by to pick up Ellie, she told me that she's been out of work for a long, long time."

"Yeah?"

"She said if she can't get a job soon, she might have to put Ellie in foster care."

"No!"

Lila nodded. "Isn't that awful? I just wish there were something I could do."

We were coming around the corner of Lila's block when we saw a big limo pull into the driveway. "Daddy's home!" she cried. She took my hand. "Come on. I've got an idea."

"A foster child!" Mr. Fowler said in surprise. "Lila, yesterday you were complaining long-distance that the children smelled bad. Now you want to adopt one?"

"I don't want us to adopt her. I just want us to give her a home for a little while. She's such a sweet little girl. She wouldn't be any trouble. And I'd take care of her."

Mr. Fowler smiled and began pulling papers out of his briefcase. "Sweetheart, a little girl isn't a puppy. A child needs constant care. Constant attention. I'm at work most of the day and you're in school."

"Mrs. Pervis is here," Lila argued.

"I hired Mrs. Pervis to be our housekeeper. Her job is to look after the house and be here with you while I'm gone. It wouldn't be fair for us to ask her to take on the responsibility of a child." He shook his head. "I'm happy to see you taking such an interest in the children at the Center. And I'm happy that you buy toys for them. But what you're asking is simply impossible. I'm sorry."

"Then maybe you could find Mrs. McMillan a job?"

Mr. Fowler smiled. "It's not that easy. There are hiring freezes in the California offices and—"

"*Daddy!* Can't you do *some*thing?"

Mr. Fowler sighed. "I'll see what I can do. But I can't promise anything. A lot of people need jobs these days. I can't hire them all—even though I wish I could."

He began flipping through papers, and then he sat down in his desk chair. "You girls run along now, OK? I've got some phone calls I need to make."

"Thanks, Daddy," Lila said softly. Then she jerked her head toward the door and I followed. We went out into the great big hallway and sat on the lowest step of the big curved marble staircase.

I love that staircase. In fact, I love the Fowler mansion. It's huge. It's bigger than the public library. And it has a ballroom, which I think is the ultimate in cool. If I had a ballroom, I'd have a ball once a week and tell everybody to wear long dresses with big fluffy skirts.

Lila sighed heavily and I squeezed her arm. "Don't get too worried. You don't know for sure that Ellie is going into foster care. Mrs. McMillan might find a job on her own. And today, you made a lot of little kids happy."

Lila nodded. "I guess so."

I hated to see Lila sad. But in a way, it was a good sign. It meant that she was starting to think about somebody besides herself.

It looked as though I wasn't the only one changing and growing up. I snuck another look at Lila. Maybe she *would* be a good president of the Unicorns.

"Forget it. No way."

"Jessica!" Mary cried the next day at lunch. "You have to go."

"I'm not going back," Jessica insisted, taking a bite of her sandwich and glowering at the rest of us as she chewed. "The kids hate me anyway," she added through a mouthful of turkey sandwich.

"No, they don't," Mary said. "Do they?" She shot a look at me and then at the rest of the group. But nobody said anything. Jessica was right. The kids didn't like her very much. Why would they? She'd really let them have it.

"Jessica, if you don't go back, we'll all get into trouble," Mary pointed out.

Jessica's face turned stony.

I sighed. Even if Jessica is my best friend, I have to admit that she can be totally stubborn, selfish, and unreasonable sometimes. And from the look on her face, this was one of those times. I was willing to bet she was feeling embarrassed for acting so awful. That's why she didn't want to go back. But that wasn't the sort of thing Jessica would ever admit.

"Remember what Mrs. Willard said," Ellen added. "They need all five of us there every afternoon."

Jessica shrugged, as if it wasn't her problem.

"Do it for the Unicorns," Mary urged.

That got her. She stopped chewing, looked at all our pleading faces, and then swallowed. "Oh, all right," she grumbled. "I'll do it for the Unicorns."

Things got off to a bad start right away that afternoon. The weather was terrible, so we decided to call Lila's dad's chauffeur, Richard, to pick us up and drive us to the Center.

He got caught in a traffic jam, and the result was that we were about twenty minutes late getting there.

By the time we arrived, the sky was black and the rain was coming down in buckets.

"Where have you been?" Mrs. Willard demanded

as soon as we walked into the playroom. She was all by herself and she looked pretty harried.

No wonder. The Wild Bunch was at it again.

Sandy and Allison had little Arthur Foo cornered, and were threatening him with Magic Markers. Mary and Ellen hurried over to break it up.

Arthur, far from being grateful, turned around and sank his teeth into Mary's arm.

"Owwwwww!" she shrieked.

Oliver laughed so hard, he fell off his stool.

"That's not funny, Oliver," Jessica scolded.

It took a while, but we finally got them rounded up and settled at the low round table. We handed out Play-Doh, and then Mary, Jessica, and I stood there with our arms crossed, ready to jump in and restore order the minute it looked as though anybody was getting out of hand.

Lila sat in the corner, rocking Ellie. We didn't have any babies today, so Ellen took charge of the two toddlers.

There was an on-edge, expectant feeling that seemed to go with the ominous weather. And when the next huge clap of thunder boomed, everybody in the room jumped.

One of the toddlers started to cry, and Yuky jumped up from the table, ran for the playhouse, and dove inside, shutting the door behind her with a bang.

"Yuky doesn't like thunder," Oliver said casually.

"Me neither," Allison said, her eyes getting big.

"Me neither," Sandy repeated.

Oliver stuck out his chest. "It doesn't bother me," he said in a show of bravado. "I'm not afraid of *anything*." He darted his eyes in Jessica's direction, and just in case we didn't get the point, stuck his tongue out at her.

Allison and Sandy began to giggle, and Arthur crossed his eyes and made a face. Then all three of them stuck their tongues out at Jessica.

Jessica scowled, but Mary reached out and took her arm. "Just ignore it," she whispered. "At least they're not fighting, biting, or screaming."

"I'm glad you're not scared," I said, sitting down at the little table with them. "Because thunder is nothing to be afraid of. It's just noise. It won't hurt anything."

Just then, there was another tremendous clap of thunder, and a big bolt of lightning came hurtling across the sky.

Keraaaacckk!

Then there was a very loud snapping sound. Every single person in the room jumped up and raced to the window just in time to see a huge branch crash to the ground.

"Oh great," I grumbled.

The door flew open, and we all turned and saw Mrs. Willard standing there with her raincoat and hat. "Girls," she said briskly, "I'm going to have to really depend on you today. Because of the weather, two of our staff members were unable to make it here. I've just had a call from my assistant. Her car is stalled at the intersection of Elm and Grove, and I'm going to have to go pick her up. That means that when I leave, there will be no one here besides yourselves."

We all looked at one another.

"Can I count on you girls to behave responsibly while I'm gone?"

"Yes, ma'am," we all said quickly.

"Please stay here and try to keep the children occupied." She suddenly stopped and turned back around. "And, girls, I haven't seen Peppermint all day. One of her favorite hiding places is in the basement. We're having trouble with the pump down there, and sometimes it floods. I've propped open the basement door with a brick so she can get out if that's where she is. But I want you girls to promise me that *none of you will go down to the basement*. And whatever you do, don't let any of the children go down there."

"Yes, ma'am," I said.

"I don't want anybody going outside, either. There's a lot of stuff blowing around out there, and it could be dangerous."

"We'll watch everybody really closely," Mary promised.

Mrs. Willard nodded. "I'll be back in about twenty minutes."

As soon as Mrs. Willard left, there was a huge clap of thunder and several of the kids began to cry. Ellen reached down, picked up Allison, and bounced her a little. "Shhhh," she whispered. "It's just thunder. Nothing's going to hurt you."

A second clap of thunder practically shook the roof.

Bam!

Yuky let out a little scream from inside the playhouse, and Arthur Foo jumped up from his chair and threw his arms around Mary's legs.

"Wow!" Mary breathed. "Look out there."

Mary picked Arthur up, and we raced to the window and saw the trees swaying and bending while the wind howled. The wind was blowing so hard that the trees were almost bent double, and the sky was turning a blackish gray.

I blew my breath out and hoped silently that Mrs. Willard would get back soon. It was going to be a very long twenty minutes.

"Where *is* she?" Ellen asked fretfully, going to the window and looking out.

It had been two and a half hours, and we hadn't heard a word from Mrs. Willard. I'd gone to call my mom to tell her I was probably going to be home late and discovered that the phones were out. No parents had arrived, which we figured meant the streets were probably flooded.

"We may be here all night," Mary said. "How are we fixed for food?"

"There are six boxes of graham crackers, two

cartons of milk, and a gallon of orange juice in the fridge," I answered.

Mary grinned. "Good. If we have to camp out here, we won't starve."

Keraaaacckk!!!

"Arrrrgggggg!" the kids all screamed.

And suddenly all the lights went out.

"Uh-oh," Jessica said.

"Calm down! Calm down!" Mary urged, clapping her hands to get their attention. "There's nothing to be afraid of. It's just a power outage."

Fortunately, there were big windows on two walls of the playroom and along the main hallway of the building. The playroom was dark but not pitch black. Of course, the windows weren't going to do us any good when it got dark outside.

"It's going to be dark soon," Ellen pointed out. "We can't stay here all night with no lights."

"That's exactly what I was thinking," I said. "Has anybody seen any candles or lamps or flashlights around?"

Oliver's hand shot up. "I have!"

"Where?"

"In the basement."

Nine

"But she said not to go in the basement," I whispered.

"She'll never know," Jessica insisted.

"Don't do it," Mary said. "It's not worth it. If Mrs. Willard finds out, we'll be out of here on our ear. She already thinks we're a bunch of losers."

"I'm not scared of Mrs. Willard," Jessica said scornfully.

"I am," I said.

"Me, too," Mary said. "Don't forget. The Unicorns are on probation. If we mess this up, Mr. Clark might ban us."

We were standing in the corner whispering so we wouldn't alarm the kids.

"The basement might be flooded," I warned. "It could be dangerous."

"Let me just go down and take a look," Jessica whispered. "Mrs. Willard left us in charge. That means she expects us to use our common sense. Right? I don't think she would expect us to sit here all night in the dark with all these terrified little kids—do you?"

When she put it that way, it made sense. I looked out the window. It was early evening and the light was going fast. In another thirty minutes, it would be dark. And it was true, I couldn't see us coping with a whole playroom full of scared, hungry kids in the dark.

"It's the only way," Jessica insisted.

I looked at her and realized what made Jessica Jessica. The rest of us were all too scared to defy Mrs. Willard, even though going to the basement was the only logical thing to do under the circumstances.

Jessica wasn't scared at all—or even if she was (and I suspected she was at least a little), she was prepared to do it anyway.

If you think about it, that's exactly the kind of person you want around in a crisis. Now I found myself thinking that Jessica would probably be a great president of the Unicorns.

"I'll go with you," I offered. And I followed her out of the playroom and down the hall to the door that led to the basement stairs.

The door was propped open a few inches with a brick and Jessica pushed it aside with her foot. She opened the door wider so we could look down the steps. Mrs. Willard was right. The basement was flooding. The floor was covered with water.

"Wow!" I whistled. "I don't think you'd better go down there."

Jessica went down a few steps and surveyed the floor. "It doesn't look deep. I'll roll up the legs of my pants," she said, stepping out of her shoes and leaning over to make cuffs. She gestured toward the four rows of freestanding metal shelves in the center of the basement. They reached up practically to the ceiling and were stacked with supplies. "I'll bet the candles are on one of those shelves."

Slowly, Jessica began tiptoeing down the wet stairs. I held the door when suddenly somebody beside me went *"Boo!"*

I was so surprised, I lost my footing and stumbled, falling sideways into Oliver.

"Hey!" he shrieked as he fell backward down the stairs.

"Yeowww!" Jessica yelled as he bumped into her and sent them both tumbling down the rest of the stairs. They landed on the floor with a splash.

"Jessica!" I shouted. "Oliver!"

"I'm OK," I heard Oliver's voice answer. Then he let out a yip, which I figured meant that Jessica was OK, too.

I was right. The next thing I knew, she was up on her feet and holding Oliver up over the water. "What do you think you're doing?" she yelled at him.

Oliver tried to twist out of her grasp. "Mrs.

Willard told you not to go down to the basement,"
he said. "I'm telling."

I could tell Jessica was seething. "Look what
you've done! You're all wet and so am I." Jessica
came trudging back up the steps.

"I'll get a blanket from the playroom," I offered.
"You can towel off before you come out."

Jessica and Oliver stood at the top of the steep
stairs, and I let go of the door and heard it shut behind me with a thud.

Uh-oh. The thud had a very permanent sound. I
put my hand on the doorknob and tried to turn it.

Nothing.

"Jessica!" I shouted. "I can't open the door from
this side. Try it from your side."

"OK!"

I heard the handle rattle as she tried to open it.
But the door didn't budge. She rattled it again. I
could feel the two of them pushing against the
door. No good.

They were locked in.

And the water was rising fast.

I hurried back to the playroom, my heart pounding. I gestured frantically for my friends to gather
around me near the door, away from where the
kids were huddled.

As soon as I had everybody's attention, I filled
them in.

"Oh, *no!*" Mary gasped. Her fingers flew to her

mouth, and even in the dim light, I could see the color drain from her face.

"Stay calm," I warned. "Everybody stay calm." My hands were shaking, but amazingly enough, my voice was steady. I knew the last thing Jessica and Oliver needed was for any of us to panic.

"We've got to do something," Lila said.

"Let's call the fire department," Ellen suggested.

"The phones are out, remember?" Lila said.

Ellen groaned. "Let's knock the door down, then," she said.

"I don't think we can. It's a steel door," I responded.

"Well, we can try," Ellen insisted. "Come on."

"Hold it," I said. "Let's try to think about this logically. Is there some other way into the basement?"

"Peppermint knows a secret way," a little voice said.

I looked down and saw that Arthur Foo had infiltrated our secret conference. He'd been hiding behind the playhouse, and I guess he'd overheard the whole conversation.

I knelt down and put my face close to his. "Peppermint has a secret way into the basement?"

Arthur nodded.

"Can you tell me?"

He shook his head.

"Can you show me?"

He paused for a minute. Then he nodded.

*　　*　　*

Lila agreed to stay with the kids, and Mary, Ellen, and I followed Arthur out into the hall, past the locked offices, and to the glass double doors of the entrance.

The weather was violent now, and between the thunder and the lightning it was like a war zone outside.

Arthur put his hands on one of the doors and started to push it open.

"Hold it," Ellen said. "He can't go out there."

"We don't have any choice." I reached up over Arthur's head and pushed the door open. Arthur blinked his eyes against the rain for a few seconds, then he began to run.

We ran behind him, following as he led us around the building toward a little potting shed constructed in the back. Behind the potting shed there were several bags piled up, waiting to be hauled away.

"Behind those bags," Arthur said.

We all began pulling the bags away, and sure enough, we found a little basement window about two feet high.

I put my fingers into the ridge at the bottom of the window and pulled, but the window was shut tight. Mrs. Willard must have closed it and locked it when the rain started.

I got down on my hands and knees and peered through the window, feeling the water pounding down on the back of my neck. I couldn't see a thing. The window was made of thick glass and it was all fogged up and wet from the weather. Besides that, it was dark in the basement.

I knocked on the window. "Jessica!" I shouted. "Can you hear me?"

I pressed my ear against the window, straining to hear an answer over the rain, but there was nothing. "*Jessica!*" I shouted again. "It's Mandy! Can you hear me?"

I crouched down, and finally, I heard a faint "I hear you."

"Are you OK?" I yelled.

"The water is up to my knees and it's rising fast. Get us out of here!" Her voice sounded as though it were coming from far away because of all the noise from the storm. It was kind of weird and eerie. Like that scene in *The Wizard of Oz* where Dorothy sees her Auntie Em in the crystal ball.

"Can you reach the window?" I yelled. "Can you open it from the inside?"

"No," she yelled. "It's about eight feet above the ground."

I sat back on my heels and blew out my breath, trying to think what to do.

Just then, there was another tremendous clap of thunder, and I felt Arthur pull away from me and dart around the building.

"Arthur, come back!" Mary shouted, starting to go after him.

"Let him go," I shouted over the pounding

rain. "It's better for him to be inside."

Mary nodded. "You're right. Now, come on. Let's see if we can get this window open."

We pushed and pushed and pushed. The water was whipping around us, and every few minutes, the sky would light up with lightning.

"Hurry!" I heard Jessica cry. "The water's rising faster."

"We can't get the window open!" I shouted.

"Break it," Mary said in a tense voice.

"How?" I gasped.

That's when I felt something tugging at the sleeve of my raincoat. I whirled around and there were Arthur, Yuky, Sandy, and Allison. Arthur was holding the brick that had propped the door open, and Sandy and Allison were holding a long jump rope.

A crack of lightning lit up the sky and illuminated their little faces. They looked scared but determined. I couldn't believe it. The Wild Bunch was riding to the rescue.

"Stand back," I ordered, taking the brick from Arthur.

Mary and Ellen herded the kids back to a safe distance.

"Stand back from the window!" I shouted through the window at Jessica and Oliver. I swung the brick.

Crash!

The window splintered, and I heard Jessica let

out a little shriek of alarm as I battered the remnants of glass out of the sill.

Once the jagged glass was cleared away, I stuck my head in the window. I could see inside the basement clearly now. It was pretty frightening. The water was swirling around the basement floor and was almost up to Jessica's thighs.

"Nice work," she said, holding up her thumb. "Let me get Oliver." She began wading away, disappearing around the steel shelving that filled the middle of the basement floor. I realized she had propped him on one of the upper shelves. All the stuff on the lower shelves had washed off, and I could see it floating around. Boxes of disposable diapers. Plastic bottles. Office supplies.

Ellen handed me the rope and I lowered it through the window. "Send Oliver up first," I yelled as Jessica came wading back around the shelves with Oliver clinging to her neck.

Jessica took the end of the rope and put it in Oliver's hands. I could see her talk to him in a low tone, explaining that he had to hold on to the rope and push away from the wall with his feet.

He nodded and looked up with big nervous eyes. I guess to a five-year-old those eight feet looked like Pike's Peak.

"I'll be right under you," she assured him. Then she looked up at me and nodded her head.

The rest of us tightened our grasp on the rope and pulled. Pretty soon, we saw Oliver's face appear at the window. He grinned when he saw us and I reached out, grabbed the back of his sweater, and pulled him through the window onto the soaking grass. Believe it or not, he began to giggle. Then he ran to the back of the rope and took a place on the tug line behind Arthur.

"OK!" Jessica yelled from inside the basement. "Pull me up."

Jessica was a lot heavier than Oliver. But with me, Ellen, Mary, Yuky, Allison, Sandy, Arthur, and Oliver, we managed to pull her up. She came crawling through the window and flopped onto the ground with a relieved groan.

Keraaaacckk!

We all dropped the rope and fell on our stomachs as a *huge* bolt of lightning split the sky.

Boom!

There was the sound of an explosion followed by a loud, angry buzzing and crackling. I lifted my head and sucked in my breath in horror.

One of the power lines had been hit, and a live wire was swaying back and forth. Sparks flew from the end of it as it whipped around against the sky like a deadly snake.

Oh no, oh no, oh no.

"Come on," I yelled, reaching out and grabbing Yuky's and Arthur's hands. "That's a live wire. Let's get back inside."

Mary grabbed Sandy up under her arm, and Ellen grabbed Allison. Jessica took Oliver's hand,

and we all dashed toward the building. We'd just reached the door when suddenly Oliver pointed toward something cowering under the swings.

"Peppermint!" he cried. Before we could say anything, he was off and running.

"*Oliver!*" Jessica screamed.

The wind began to blow and the live wire came swinging in Oliver's direction.

"OLIVER!" Ellen and Mary shrieked.

Jessica dashed across the yard after him. With one swift movement, she dove forward, tackled him, and then rolled away to safety just as the electrical wire came whipping over their heads.

My heart was pounding so hard, I could hear the blood drumming in my ears. If the wire had swung two inches lower, they both would have been electrocuted.

"Come back!" Mary screeched.

"Let me go!" Oliver shouted, struggling in her arms as Jessica came running back toward the building.

"Here," she panted, shoving him at Mary.

"No!" Mary protested when she realized what Jessica was planning to do. "Get back here!"

But Jessica paid no attention. She dashed back toward the swings.

"Noooo!" I yelled.

"Jessica, don't do it!" Ellen shrieked.

Typical Jessica. She was going back for Peppermint even though it was crazy, dangerous, and so stupid that my fingers itched to wring her neck.

She paused, just out of range, and watched the wind whip the wire back and forth, back and forth, in front of the swings. Poor Peppermint cowered on the ground, watching it with big, saucerlike eyes.

"I can't watch," Ellen moaned.

"I can't believe she's doing this," Mary breathed.

"Go inside!" I ordered the kids.

But before they could obey, the wind changed direction and whipped the wire backward. Jessica seized her chance. Quicker than the lightning, she reached out, grabbed Peppermint by the back of the neck, and yanked her to safety.

My legs were wobbling by the time Jessica came jogging back toward us with Peppermint in her arms and a big smile on her face.

"Hooray!" the kids all yelled, running toward Jessica to pet the trembling cat.

A few minutes later we were all in the playroom, laughing and shouting, drying ourselves off with paper towels, and wrapping ourselves up in blankets.

Lila had a million questions, and every kid except Yuky wanted to be the one to tell the story of the amazing rescue of Oliver and Jessica, and how Jessica had saved Peppermint.

Suddenly, we saw Ellen's eyes grow huge and she let out a little shriek.

Bang! went the double doors as they flew open and hit the walls on either side.

We all whirled around.

Mrs. Willard was standing there with her hands on her hips and rain dripping off the brim of her rain hat. Beside her stood Mr. and Mrs. Foo and Ms. Ridley, her assistant.

Mrs. Willard looked furious. "What happened?" she demanded. "I left you girls in charge. I gave you specific instructions not to go outside! Obviously, you have disobeyed me."

I could feel my hands shaking. We were in trouble. Really big trouble.

Jessica swallowed, then she stepped forward. "It was my fault," she said in a level voice. "It was all my fault."

Mrs. Willard's lips tightened and she stared at Jessica for a long moment. "All right, then, Jessica. I intend to call Mr. Clark tonight and inform him that you are unreliable and irresponsible and that the Center would prefer that you not return."

"No!" protested a little voice. And before anybody could say another word, Oliver stepped forward. "It wasn't Jessica's fault, Mrs. Willard. It was mine."

Mrs. Willard's eyes darted back and forth between Jessica and Oliver, like she was trying to make up her mind who to believe.

Then Arthur Foo stepped in front of Jessica, too. "It was my fault," he said softly.

"My fault, too," Sandy and Allison said in unison, stepping in front of Jessica.

Yuky didn't say anything. But she let go of my hand and stepped in front of Jessica along with the others.

It was quite a sight, Jessica standing there soaking wet, with a wet cat in her arms, and surrounded by wet children.

"Sandy! Allison!" A lady appeared behind Mrs. Willard wrapped in a raincoat and carrying a huge umbrella.

"Mommy!" they shouted, running past Mrs. Willard and throwing themselves into their mother's arms.

Immediately, the mood was broken. Everybody was talking at once. Explaining and apologizing. And Mrs. Willard just didn't have the chance to yell at us anymore, although I could tell she wanted to.

"I'm so sorry to be late," Mrs. Meyer panted. "I've been sitting in traffic for two hours. They just opened up East Boulevard, so I could finally get through."

"I know," Mrs. Willard said. "I just got here myself—"

She broke off in surprise as the lights came on. We ran to the window and saw the Light and Power truck outside.

"They're repairing the lines already," Mary said.

The door opened again, and Mr. Johnson, Oliver's dad, and several other parents came in. They'd all been stranded at the end of the boulevard.

Mrs. Willard went immediately to her office to call somebody about the basement, and the rest of us helped bundle up the kids in their jackets.

It was dark by the time the last toddler had been picked up. Lila called her house from the pay phone and asked Richard, their chauffeur, to come get us.

As we walked by Mrs. Willard's office, she was still sitting there talking on the phone. We said goodnight, but I don't think she heard us, because she never even looked up or waved goodbye.

Ten

That night, my mom, Archie, and Cecelia listened in amazement to my story of the double rescue. The rescue of Jessica and Oliver. And then Jessica's display of heroism on behalf of Oliver and Peppermint.

Archie, especially, was full of questions. Mostly about Peppermint. How old was Peppermint. How big? What color?

After a late dinner of roast chicken and potatoes, we all watched the news and saw that the storm had been the worst one Sweet Valley had seen in ten years.

They didn't have to convince me. I'd been there.

The Child Care Center was closed for the next two days so the basement could be pumped out.

The bad weather lasted through the next weekend, which was OK with me. The Center had been taking up a lot of my free time, and I needed to get caught up on my schoolwork. It's always easier for me to stay inside and study on rainy days than it is on sunny days.

Everybody else must have been hitting the books that weekend, too, because as far as I know, there weren't any Unicorn get-togethers.

Jessica and Elizabeth went with their parents to watch their brother play basketball on Saturday and spent all day Sunday studying. Ellen spent most of the weekend at the library, because she had a big research paper due. And Mary went with her parents on Sunday to visit her grandmother.

Monday morning was really busy, and I didn't get to the cafeteria until fifteen minutes before lunch was over. All I had time to do was grab an apple and a carton of milk and wave to the Unicorns before I headed off to class.

I aced my history test fifth period and got back my math homework with an A-plus on it sixth period. So by the time I met up with the rest of the Unicorns after school, I was in a good mood.

"Well?" Ellen said, as we stood on the front steps. "What do you think? Are we still supposed to go to the Center? Has Mrs. Willard talked to Mr. Clark yet?"

Jessica chewed on her thumbnail. "Mr. Clark didn't say anything to me today about me not going back. Did he say anything to anybody else?"

Every head shook from side to side.

"Then I say let's go," Lila said, hoisting her backpack up on her shoulder. "If Mrs. Willard doesn't want us, she can tell us to go away."

"Jessicaaaa!"

As soon as we reached the door, the Wild Bunch came running over to Jessica. It was amazing. She'd gone from being Playroom Enemy Number One to being their hero.

All of them were clamoring for her attention at once. Arthur wanted to show her some baseball cards, and Allison and Sandy had learned a new joke they wanted to tell her.

Oliver was taking a very proprietary position, since *he* had been the one in the basement with Jessica.

"Miss Wakefield!"

We all turned and saw Mrs. Willard standing there smiling at us.

I was amazed. I'd never seen her smile before. She looked almost . . . nice.

"I understand I owe you an apology," she said. "I'm glad to see you're back. Elizabeth came by at lunch today and explained to me what happened," she continued. "I want to thank you for your initiative and courage. You set a good example for the children. But next time," her face fell into a frown, "please do not risk your life for a cat."

She reached down and picked up Peppermint, who let out a loud *purrrrrr*. "The cat has nine lives and you only have one."

After that, things at the Center went smoothly. We had no problems at all. Our big adventure seemed to have changed everything. We bonded; what can I say?

We didn't have any more setbacks until the middle of our second week—the afternoon when Lila and I came into the playroom and she noticed immediately that Ellie wasn't there.

"Mrs. Willard," Lila asked, bustling over to the kitchen area. "Where's Ellie? Is she sick?"

Mrs. Willard motioned to us to step over behind the counter, where she was checking the graham cracker inventory. "Mrs. McMillan took Ellie for an interview with Foster Care Services today," she said in a low tone.

"Oh, no!" Lila and I both cried.

Mrs. Willard reached up and pulled down a box of graham crackers and shook her head sadly. "I'm afraid so. She hasn't had any luck finding a job. The situation is becoming very difficult. If she doesn't find one soon, she'll have to leave Sweet Valley and try another city. If she does, Ellie will have to go to a foster home until Mrs. McMillan gets herself settled."

"That's horrible!" Lila protested. "I'm going to talk to my father again. He's got to do something."

Mrs. Willard smiled. "I'm sure Mrs. McMillan would be grateful for any help he could give. But, girls, I don't want you to think that foster care is permanent. And it's not necessarily a bad thing. Besides," she said briskly, "it might not even come to that."

I knew that Mrs. Willard was right about foster care. Mary had been a foster child once. She had loved her foster parents and still went to visit them sometimes.

Still, I couldn't help thinking how awful it would be for a child as young as Ellie to be separated from her mother. I was a lot older than Ellie, and if somebody told me tomorrow that I couldn't live with my mom anymore, I'd be heartbroken. I don't think I could take it.

I hoped Mrs. Willard was right. I hoped it wouldn't come to that.

"'Bye, Mrs. Willard," we all chorused.

It was five-thirty in the evening, two days later, and we were all filing down the hall on our way out of the Center. As we walked by the open door of Mrs. Willard's office, we all waved.

"See you next week," Mary said.

Mrs. Willard came out into the hall and smiled. "No you won't."

We all looked at one another. What was she talking about?

"Your thirty hours are up today," she explained.

"They are?"

"Are you sure?"

"No way," I insisted.

"Four hours every weekday afternoon for eight days. By my calculations, that's thirty-two hours," Mrs. Willard said.

I couldn't believe it. I was suddenly overcome by the realization that I didn't want our thirty hours to be over. I felt as though we'd just gotten settled into the place. I felt that we were just getting to know everybody. And in a certain way, I felt that we were just getting to know ourselves.

Mrs. Willard went over to her desk and returned with a piece of paper. "See? I kept a chart. Thirty-two hours. You're free."

Nobody said anything for a long time.

"All right!" Ellen said from the back. But it didn't sound too convincing.

We shook hands all around, and Mrs. Willard thanked us again for all our help.

And seconds later we were standing outside, blinking at one another in the bright sunlight.

"Free at last," Jessica said.

"No more diapers," Mary sighed.

"No more graham crackers and milk," I pointed out.

Everybody was trying to put on a good act—but nobody sounded very convincing. I could tell they all felt the same way I did.

"I say this calls for a celebration," Mary said,

trying to get everybody's spirits going. "Let's have a party. The Unicorns are finally free."

"We'll have it at my house," Lila immediately volunteered. "And hey . . . I just had a crazy idea."

"Let's invite the kids!" we all said at once. Then we started laughing.

"Mrs. Willard!" we shouted, running back into the Center to get her permission.

"We'll need a cake and some ice cream," Mary said, resting her elbows on the table and scraping the bottom of her yogurt container with a spoon.

"What about entertainment?" Lila asked, tapping her fountain pen against the edge of her notebook.

We were sitting around the huge kitchen of the Fowler mansion. We had been so excited about giving a party that instead of going home after leaving the Center, we had gone straight over to Lila's house to start planning. You see, the Unicorns love throwing parties. And we hadn't had one in a while.

Lila had passed out yogurt and cookies and sodas and then we'd gotten to work, trying to make a list of the things we were going to need to throw a really good kids' party.

The party was going to be on Sunday. Mrs. Willard had agreed to make arrangements with the parents to drop the kids off at the Center on Sunday morning. Then she and a couple of the staff members would drive them all over to the Fowlers' in the Center's van. After the party, Mrs. Willard would take the kids back to the Center, where their parents would pick them up.

"For entertainment, they can play Pin the Tail on the Donkey," I said.

"But they play that at the Center," Lila argued.

Mary shrugged. "Yeah. And they like it. So why not let them play it at the party?"

Lila shook her head. "Parties should be special occasions," she said. "If you do the same old thing at a party that you do every day, then it's not anything special. I want to be sure they have a good time. I want them to have a day they'll never forget."

"Lila!" Mary exclaimed. "They're little kids. All they need to have a good time is a Popsicle and a garden hose."

"She's right," I said. "In fact, that's not a bad idea. Let's tell them to wear bathing suits under their shorts. That way if it's warm enough, they can play with the hose. Archie and I used to love playing in the hose. Kids love anything wet—hoses, puddles, ditches."

I noticed Lila got this funny look on her face—half appalled and half skeptical. "Really?"

"Sure," Mary said with a grin.

"But we have a *pool*," Lila pointed out. "Why would they want to fool around with a hose when they can go in the pool?"

"It's OK with me if it's OK with Mrs. Willard," Mary said. "But I'll bet she won't want the kids to go anywhere near the pool unless we have a lifeguard."

"Elizabeth has taken lifesaving," Jessica said. "I'll bet she'll come and help out. I'll ask her tonight."

"OK," Lila said briskly. She put the cap on her fountain pen. "I've got the picture." She nodded her head several times. "Leave it to me. I'll take care of everything. Mrs. Pervis will help me."

"That's not fair," I protested. "We don't want you to do all the work and buy all the food."

"That's right," Mary echoed.

Even though Lila has tons of money, we try really hard not to take advantage of her. I think I mentioned before that our parents are all pretty adamant about it. They say we should all pay our own share and our own way. Otherwise, Lila would never know whether we're her friends because we like her or because she has lots of money.

Also, my mom makes kind of a big deal about not borrowing things from Lila—or one another, for that matter.

Lila's offered to lend me clothes a bunch of times, but my mom won't let me take her up on it unless it's something I can afford to replace out of my own allowance if something happens to it. That means that, basically, I can borrow Lila's socks if I want to.

"We figured the refreshments should cost about ten dollars apiece," Jessica said, paging back to the front of her notebook. "That's if we use coupons."

Mary opened her purse and pulled out a little sheaf of coupons. We were always collecting them for our party fund, and Mary held on to them because she's our treasurer. "We've got coupons for chips, ice cream, sodas, and paper napkins."

"OK," Lila said agreeably. "Why don't you guys give me the money and the coupons and I'll give them to Mrs. Pervis. Then she can order the refreshments when she places our regular grocery order. OK?"

Everybody agreed to that. We all gave Lila our ten dollars, volunteered to bring various board games and toys, and then took off.

That Sunday, when Jessica and I arrived at Lila's to start helping her get ready, there were two or three huge trucks parked outside the Fowler mansion.

"What's going on?" I asked Jessica.

She shrugged. "Maybe Mr. Fowler is having some work done on the house."

"Oh, no. I hope it doesn't mess up our party," I said.

"Me, too," Jessica said, ringing the doorbell.

We could hear the bell chime deep inside the house, but nobody answered.

"That's funny." I peered in the side windows and didn't see any signs of life.

Just then, there was this strange, shrill, trumpeting sound from behind the house.

"What was that?" I yelped.

"Workmen, maybe?"

I just shook my head. It didn't sound mechanical. But it didn't sound quite human, either. I suddenly pictured aliens holding the Fowlers hostage in the backyard.

Before my imagination could crank into overdrive, the door opened and we both gasped. It wasn't Lila, Mr. Fowler, Mrs. Pervis, or aliens who answered the door.

It was a clown. A clown on stilts.

"Sandy and Allison, I presume?" he said in a funny voice.

Jessica began to laugh and so did I.

"Not exactly," she said, giggling. "I'm Jessica Wakefield and this is Mandy Miller."

"Unicorns!" he exclaimed. "I *love* Unicorns. Come in!"

He backed up into the front hall so we could come in and motioned to us to follow him through the foyer. It was a good thing the ceilings in Lila's house were so high, or his head would have been scraping the ceiling. As it was, he just barely cleared the chandelier. "Miss Fowler is in the back with her father and the household staff," he explained as he moved swiftly through the house on his stilts. "It seems there's been a slight problem with the elephant."

Jessica and I looked at each other.

Elephant?

Eleven

Having an incredibly rich friend can sometimes be a big pain. I mean, you always know that no matter what you do, you can never compete.

But when that rich friend decides to put her money and her imagination to work making other people happy—well, then having a rich friend is the best thing in the whole world.

And that's the way I felt about the party. I'd never felt so proud of Lila in my whole life. Sure, she'd gotten a little carried away, but she'd obviously spent a lot of time thinking about those kids and what would make them happy.

"Carried away?" Lila said, her mouth open in surprise, when I teased her about it. "What makes you think I got carried away?"

Jessica began to laugh. "Oh, nothing," she said,

shaking her head. "I guess this is just your average kids' party." She smiled at me. "It's amazing what you can get for sixty dollars, isn't it?"

"It was the coupons that made it all possible," Lila said, and she laughed.

The three of us were standing by the enormous refreshment table watching the fun. We may have been teasing Lila, but nobody was complaining. The kids were having a great time. *Everybody* was having a great time. Including me.

Not only was there a clown on stilts, there was a clown juggler, a clown lifeguard, a clown magician, and two clown musicians playing banjos.

On top of that, there was a baby elephant for the kids to ride. And best of all, Lila had rented one of those huge water slides set up so that you could slide right down into the pool.

"You said kids liked anything wet," she said with a big grin.

And boy, did they.

We looked up just in time to see Oliver come hurtling down the water slide and—*splash!*—land in the arms of the lifeguard clown. The lifeguard paddled over to the side of the pool, helped Oliver out, and then swam back in time to catch Sandy as she came whizzing down.

"Watch me, Mandy!" Arthur yelled as he hurried up the steps of the slide.

Lila had also invited Elizabeth and Maria to help out with the party. They were having a great time, and I could tell how surprised they were at the relationships we had formed with the kids. Elizabeth didn't say anything, but I knew her respect for the Unicorns grew a lot that afternoon.

Lila had called a catering service to do the refreshments, and you never saw food like this in your life. Waiters in white coats passed peanut butter and jelly sandwiches on silver trays—peanut butter and jelly sandwiches that were cut in the shape of airplanes and stars.

A long table had been set up on the patio, and a big crystal punch bowl in the center held foaming ice cream float. Up and down the table there were platters of cupcakes and cookies.

For the grownups, like Mrs. Willard and Mr. Fowler, there was caviar and pâté.

I tasted the pâté, which wasn't completely horrible, and the caviar, which was the nastiest stuff I have ever put in my mouth. I think I said something a while back about growing up and maturing. Forget I said that. I take it back. One bite of caviar sent me running for a peanut butter and jelly sandwich and a big swallow of ice cream float.

"Come on, Mandy," Allison yelled as she climbed out of the pool. "Ride the elephant."

"I'll be right there," I called out. I was looking around, mentally ticking off who was where. I saw Sandy and Ellie going up the steps of the water slide while Lila and Mary cheered them on.

I saw Arthur Foo and the juggler playing a wild

game of catch in which new balls kept appearing from the juggler's sleeve.

Oliver and Jessica came running over to the refreshment table after a trip down the water slide.

But I didn't see Yuky anywhere.

Then I heard a familiar giggle.

I leaned over, picked up the edge of the table-cloth, and saw Yuky grinning at me from underneath the table. "What are you doing under there?" I teased.

She smiled.

"Want to come out and ride the elephant with me?"

She chewed a little while on the edge of a cookie while she thought it over, then she grinned and came crawling out. She took my hand and we hurried over to the side of the yard, where a lot of the kids were lined up for elephant rides. Right at the head of the line was Mr. Fowler. He was holding Ellie in his arms.

For some reason, Ellie just had an irresistible attraction to the Fowlers. She looked thrilled to death to be with Mr. Fowler, and the feeling was clearly mutual.

"She looks just like Lila did when she was little," he said, smiling at me. Then he bounced Ellie a little in his arms.

Ellie gave a delighted squeal and Mr. Fowler laughed. "Mandy, I think the Unicorns did a wonderful thing here today. You girls are turning out to be very admirable young ladies."

"It was Lila who put all this together," I said. "The rest of us were planning to give them Popsicles and a garden hose. It was Lila's idea to give them a day they would never forget."

He nodded and put Ellie up on the baby elephant's back. "I know," he said, belting Ellie into the seat so that she wouldn't slide off. "But I'm talking about more than just today. You girls have changed. I don't think Lila would have thought of doing something like this a few weeks ago."

Lila and I volunteered to ride back to the Center in the van after the party. We knew Mrs. Willard was going to need some help getting the kids unloaded and sent home with the right towels and toys.

Lila and I sat in the backseat with Ellie between us. Oliver, Arthur, Allison, and Sandy sat in the very back. Yuky sat in the front seat. She kept turning around to peek at me over the back of the seat. I couldn't help wondering if we were destined to part without her ever saying a word to me.

When we pulled into the parking lot of the Center, most of the parents were already there. Mr. Johnson and Mrs. Foo were standing in the shade of a tree when all the kids started piling out.

"Dad! Dad!" Oliver shouted, running toward his father.

Mr. Johnson picked Oliver up and swung him

around. "Hey, there. Did you have fun at the party?"

"It was unbelievable!" Oliver breathed. "We got there and there was this big mansion, just like on TV. And they had an elephant. And a water slide just like the one at Water Wonder Works."

Mr. Johnson smiled. "Is that so?" he said in an interested voice. "Sounds to me like you were at the White House."

Oliver shook his head. "The White House is in Washington. Besides, this was more like a castle."

Mr. Johnson winked at me, and I could tell he thought Oliver was exaggerating. Who could blame him? If I'd never seen the Fowlers' Georgian-style mansion, I wouldn't believe it either. I didn't have time to explain, though. Mr. Johnson was in a hurry to get home, so he thanked us and then led Oliver to the car. I could hear Oliver's excited voice talking a mile a minute all the way across the parking lot: "A real elephant . . . and a pool . . . sandwiches in the shape of stars . . ."

Allison and Sandy's grandmother picked them up, and Yuky's teenage brother came for her.

Finally, the only people left were me, Lila, Mrs. Willard, and Ellie. We leaned against the car, watching the road.

Ellie began to worry a little, turning and twisting impatiently. "Where's my mommy?" she asked.

"She'll be here," Lila assured her. "In the meantime, we'll sit here together. OK?"

Ellie let out a plaintive little whine. "I want my mommy."

I squatted down so that my face was level with hers. "She's just a little late, Ellie. But she'll be here. Don't worry."

She didn't say anything, but she didn't look completely convinced either. I wondered if she had sensed that things might be about to change—that she might be losing her mommy for a while—and maybe that was why she was suddenly so anxious.

It made me want to wrap my arms around her and tell her that everything was going to be all right. That she and her mommy would always be together. But I knew I couldn't do that. It might not be true.

I stood up quickly because I felt a lump forming in my throat.

Lila looked as though she was having a few private, worried thoughts of her own. She picked up Ellie and held her close.

We waited a few more minutes, leaning against the car, feeling the late-afternoon breeze ruffle our hair and watching it blow the tall weeds back and forth in the yard. After all the excitement of Lila's party, there was an abandoned, lonely feeling about the Center that afternoon.

Mrs. Willard was just looking at her watch when we saw Mrs. McMillan's old car pull into the parking lot.

"Mommy!" Ellie shrieked. She wriggled out of

Lila's grasp and started running toward the car.

It was like the sun coming out after a rainy day. Seeing Ellie squealing with happiness and running toward her mother chased away the lonely feeling. And every face was smiling.

Mrs. McMillan got out, scooped Ellie up in a hug, and came hurrying over full of apologies. "I am so sorry to be late," she said. "I had another job interview. It was on the other side of town, and it took me a lot longer to get back than I thought it would."

"An interview?" Lila smiled. "That's great. How did it go?"

Mrs. McMillan sighed. "Well. They liked me, and I liked them, but I don't know. It's a retail store, which is why I had an interview on Sunday. They're open seven days a week. If I went to work there, I'd be working weekends. I'm not sure what I would do with Ellie."

"We would take turns baby-sitting," Lila said quickly. "Right, Mandy?"

I nodded. "Sure we would."

Mrs. McMillan smiled. "You girls are really wonderful, and I'll keep that in mind. But I don't know whether I'll get the job or not. I don't have exactly the kind of experience they're looking for."

"When will you find out?" Lila asked.

"Probably tomorrow or Tuesday."

"I'll keep my fingers crossed for you," Mrs.

Willard said, as Mrs. McMillan put Ellie down and began leading her toward the car.

"Thanks." Mrs. McMillan smiled. "I need all the help I can get."

As I watched them climb into their car and drive away, I crossed my fingers for luck. I crossed them so hard, it made my knuckles ache—almost as much as my heart.

Twelve

"Isn't this where we started?" Mary asked with a laugh.

"It's exactly where we started," Ellen said, leaning back and hanging her feet over the armrests of the big chair in the Wakefields' living room. "Who's going to be president?"

It was Monday, after school, and it was as if somebody had rewound a tape. Just as Mary said, we were back where we had started. Jessica and Lila were sitting on the sofa, I was sprawled in a wing chair, and Mary was lying across a footstool on her stomach, munching on cheddar-cheese popcorn.

We were holding a special session of the Unicorns, because we hadn't held a real old-fashioned Unicorn meeting in over three weeks. And we still hadn't resolved the matter of who was going to be president.

"Does either of the presidential candidates wish to withdraw?" I asked hopefully. If one of them changed her mind about wanting the job, it sure would make life easier.

"Not me," Jessica replied cheerfully.

"Me either," Lila chimed in with a grin.

Oh, well. I knew it couldn't be that easy.

"Should we have another dare war?" Ellen asked.

"*No!*" everybody shouted in unison. Then we began to laugh.

"Then how are we going to settle this?" Ellen demanded.

I cleared my throat and stood. "I propose we get our president the old-fashioned way—by election. We have two good candidates. Jessica, whose quick thinking, bravery, and heroism have proven her to be a capable leader. And Lila, whose generosity, selfless philanthropy, and creative talents make her not only an asset to her friends and her school but to the community as a whole."

"Hear! Hear!" Mary said in a phony English accent.

Jessica and Lila collapsed on the couch in giggles.

"Speech! Speech!" Ellen hooted.

Jessica stood up. "Lila's a great friend. A great Unicorn. And a great party giver. She'd be a great president. But vote for me anyway."

Everybody laughed and applauded.

Then Lila stood up. "Jessica's just about the coolest

person I know. But I still want to be president."

Everybody laughed again and Lila popped back up. "And while I've got the floor, I want to ask everyone if they would like to plan a zoo outing for the kids at the Center."

"Sounds great," Mary said, passing the bag of popcorn to Lila.

Lila took some popcorn. "The man who brought the elephant to the party works at the zoo. He told me that two weeks from Saturday, the zoo is going to have a kids' day. They're going to have tons of baby animals for kids to pet or ride. Admission is free," she added. "The only thing we'd have to pay for is some refreshments." Lila grinned and tossed a popcorn kernel at Mary. "And this time they really will have to settle for Popsicles."

Mary opened her mouth, but the kernel hit her smack in the middle of her forehead. "Count me in," she said, laughing. "It sounds like fun."

"Me, too," Ellen said.

"Me, three," Jessica said.

"I think it sounds great," I added.

"I'll call Mrs. Willard about getting the parents' permission," Lila said. "And if she can't drive us in the school van, I'm sure my dad will let us use the company stretch limo. It'll seat everybody and it's got plenty of safety belts."

I almost couldn't believe it was Lila talking. It was as though she had undergone a real personality change. A change for the better. And it was all because of Ellie. Somehow, Ellie had touched her heart. Lila had never had to think about anybody else in her whole life. And now she was finding out that making other people happy could be fun.

"There's only one thing that's worrying me about the kids' day," I said.

Everybody looked at me.

"The zoo is going to be really crowded. We've never taken the kids anywhere where we might lose them. Maybe this is too ambitious."

"That's a good point," Jessica said. "You know the minute they get there, they're going to go running off in six different directions."

"When I was in foster care," Mary said, "there was once a bunch of kids in the same house. Most of us were really young. Our foster mom used to always wear a bright red blouse with yellow sleeves when she took us somewhere. You couldn't miss that blouse. She trained us always to look for the blouse if we got lost. It worked really well."

"I have a red and yellow blouse," Ellen offered.

I pulled the end of my braid and brushed it back and forth across my lips. "I see what you're saying," I told Mary. "But for that to work, we'd all have to have the same kind of blouse, and I don't think we all want to run out and buy matching blouses. Maybe we could all tie a balloon to our wrists. I saw a tour guide do that once at a museum."

"No good," Jessica said. "*Everybody* at the zoo has a balloon."

"Why don't we just all wear something purple?" Ellen suggested with a shrug. "If there's one thing we've all got, it's purple clothes."

"What if we got club jackets?" Lila suggested, her eyes lighting up. "Maybe . . . purple satin, like baseball jackets, with sequined unicorns on the back. You couldn't miss those in a crowd."

"That would be so cool!" I said.

Everybody else whistled and applauded.

"Who wants to volunteer to find out about getting jackets?" I asked.

I raised my hand and everybody applauded again. This was right up my alley. I loved clothes and I especially loved funky clothes.

The next twenty minutes were taken up with discussions about jackets and prices and kids and permission slips, and before we knew it, Mr. Wakefield came walking in the door from work and it was time for us all to go home.

As I was walking back to my house, I remembered that we still hadn't settled the question of a president. But strangely enough, we didn't seem to need one right now.

We were a club, but we had also become a team. A group of people with common goals and a desire to work together to make them happen. And we were also having more fun than we had ever had before.

We'd come a long way from the competitive, gossiping, mean group of girls who had started a dare war.

*   *   *

"It feels strange not to have to go to the Center this afternoon," Mary said on Monday at lunch.

"Strange but kind of nice," Ellen said.

I poked at my lasagna. "I like having afternoons to myself again," I said. "I love the kids, but not every day."

"That's for sure," Jessica agreed.

"Maybe now we can finally get the Booster Club going again," Ellen suggested. "Now that we're in seventh grade, the football team will be much more fun to cheer for."

Lila nodded. "And I've got a ton of shopping to catch up on." She laughed as she picked up her goat cheese and sun-dried tomato sandwich. "I wore the same outfit twice last week."

"I'd love to do a little shopping myself," I said. I'd seen in the paper that there was a new thrift store opening up. Being an avid thrift-store shopper, I couldn't wait to get over there and check it out.

"No more spilled milk and smooshed crackers," Mary said.

"No more finger paints," Ellen said.

"No more Oliver." Jessica grinned.

"Oh, go on," we all teased. Jessica and Oliver were regular valentines these days.

"So," I asked Jessica, "want to check out the new thrift store with me this afternoon?"

"Uhhhh, better count me out. I've got some stuff I need to do."

"Mary?"

"Ummmm, I better not. I told my mom I'd come right home."

I asked Ellen and even Lila.

Hmmmm. No takers. That was OK.

I was actually slightly relieved. It meant I could drop by the Child Care Center on my way to the thrift store. Believe it or not, I was missing the kids. I know I said I was glad to have a free afternoon, but what was one little visit?

Still, I didn't want my friends to know what I was planning. Dropping by the Center just to say hello on my first free afternoon seemed kind of, well . . . *geeky.*

"*What are you doing here?*" Mary and I both demanded at the same time.

I had been coming around the corner on my way to the playroom and bumped smack into Mary, who had been coming full speed around the corner from the opposite direction.

"I thought you told your mom you were going right home," I squeaked, feeling my nose to make sure it was still on straight.

Her face turned pink. "I, uhhh, thought I might have left a library book here," she explained weakly. She patted her nose and then examined her hand to make sure it wasn't bleeding. It wasn't. "I thought *you* said you were going to the new thrift store," she said suspiciously.

"I, ummm, couldn't find my green sweater. I thought maybe I'd find it here."

Mary lowered her hand and gave me a knowing smile. "Yeah. Right. Why couldn't you just admit you wanted to drop by and see the kids?"

"Why couldn't you?" I countered with a grin.

"I didn't want everyone to think I was . . ."

"Geeky?" I finished for her.

She grinned. "Exactly. Jessica and Lila would tease us mercilessly if they knew."

"I won't tell anybody we were here if you won't."

Mary stuck out her hand and we shook. "Deal."

"Come on," I said in a conspiratorial voice.

The two of us hurried on down the hall toward the playroom. As soon as we'd pushed open the doors, we started laughing. The Wild Bunch was as wild as ever. Oliver was standing on a table singing a hip-hop version of "Itsy Bitsy Spider" while Allison, Sandy, and Yuky stood behind him and made motions with their hands.

As soon as Allison and Sandy saw us, they smiled and waved and really started to ham it up, moving their hands around to show us the spider crawling up the water spout and stamping their feet as if they were stomping bugs.

Elizabeth was sitting on the kitchen counter, and she gave us a big grin. "I'm glad you guys are here," she said, reaching back to tuck a stray hair into her ponytail. "I think you're better at keeping them quiet than I am."

Mary lifted Oliver down off the table, and I began to herd Allison, Sandy, and Yuky down before they broke the table in half.

"Well, what do you know!" Mary said, laughing and pointing to the door. "Mandy and I weren't the only ones who couldn't stay away."

Ellen was standing in the door, blinking in surprise. "What are you guys doing here?"

"The same thing you're doing here," I countered. "And the same thing Jessica is doing here." I pointed to the kitchen area.

Mary started making her motorboat noise.

"I'm not Jessica, I'm Elizabeth!" the Wakefield twin insisted.

We all started laughing. "Your Elizabeth impression is pretty good, Jess," I said, "but you can't fool your best friends."

Oliver came screaming over with his hands in the air. "Jessicaaaa!"

"And you can't fool Oliver, either."

Jessica smiled, and sheepishly pulled the scrunchy from her ponytail. "OK, OK. You got me."

"Let's face it, you guys," Mary said. "Great Unicorn minds think alike."

That's when Mrs. Willard walked in with a sack full of groceries. She smiled when she saw us. "Well, well, well. If it isn't the Chain Gang."

We laughed. How did Mrs. Willard know we called ourselves that?

"Lila called me about the kids' day at the zoo,"

she said with a smile. "I've told the children and they're very excited. Aren't you?"

Oliver jumped in the air and screamed. All the other kids jumped up in imitation.

"Girls," she said, motioning us over to the counter. "I just wanted you to know that I'm drafting a letter to Mr. Clark to let him know what a wonderful job you've done here. He had warned me that I might be getting a group of spoiled, smart-alecky girls who wouldn't be of much help. I want him to know that he was absolutely wrong."

That gave me goose bumps, it was so nice. I swallowed. "Thanks, Mrs. Willard."

"Thank you," Jessica, Mary, and Ellen chimed in.

"Hey," Mary said, looking around. "Where's Ellie?"

Mrs. Willard's face tightened. "Well, uh, as we anticipated, Mrs. McMillan went to Los Angeles to look for a job."

My heart sank. "You mean . . ."

Mrs. Willard nodded her head. "That's right. I'm afraid she's had to put Ellie in a foster home."

Mary's face froze into a mask and she turned away. I guess for Mary it felt almost like going through it herself all over again. Losing her mom. Losing her home.

Jessica put her arm around Mary's shoulders. Ellen hung her head. I gazed at the empty rocking chair where Lila and Ellie usually sat, having no idea at all what to say. It was too sad.

That's when the door opened and Lila came bopping in. She had sunglasses on and a little wrapped box in her hands. She paused in surprise when she saw us, then she smiled. "Hi. What's everybody doing here?"

Mary lifted her eyes and threw the rest of us a horrified look. We knew how upset Lila was going to be about Ellie. Which one of us was going to tell her?

"Hey!" Lila giggled. "Are you guys playing the quiet game or something?"

Bam!

The door of the playhouse burst open and out came the Wild Bunch. Oliver, Allison, Sandy, Arthur, and Yuky. They were giggling and began running laps around the playroom.

"If you guys are playing the quiet game," Lila said with a laugh, "you're not doing it very well." Then her eyes flickered over the group and she frowned. Her lips seemed to be ticking off the names, taking the roll.

She leaned over and peeked inside the playhouse, as if she was checking to see if there was anybody else in there. Then she straightened up and looked around the room again. She looked over at us with a wary, puzzled expression.

"Where's Ellie?"

Thirteen

"That's a great sweater," Lois Waller said to Lila the next morning when we were standing around our lockers before homeroom. "It's exactly the kind of thing I need to go with my new skirt. Where did you get it?"

Lila's lip lifted in a sneer, and I felt my stomach tighten up. I hadn't seen that look on Lila's face in a long time. Not since last year, when she was doing her constant Janet Howell imitation. "Gee, Lois," Lila said in a really sarcastic voice. "I don't think it comes in size gigantic. And even if it did, I doubt if you could afford a sweater like this."

Lois recoiled as if she had been slapped.

Mary gasped and shut her locker with an angry bang. "Lila!" she said sharply.

"Yes?" Lila said in a breathy voice. She gave

Mary a fake wide-eyed innocent look.

"I'm sorry, Lois," I said in a low tone. I reached out to put my hand on her arm, but she yanked it away.

"For some reason, I thought maybe the Unicorns had changed," Lois said in a hurt voice. "I was trying to give you guys the benefit of the doubt. But you're just as snobby as ever."

"Lois!" Mary and I both called out as she hurried away.

But Lois disappeared into her classroom and never even looked back.

"Nice work, Fowler," Mary said angrily.

Lila just shrugged. "I don't care what Lois Waller thinks. Besides, Mary, it's beneath the dignity of any Unicorn to care what the school fat girl thinks."

I couldn't believe it. I couldn't believe how awful Lila was being.

"Is it beneath the dignity of a Unicorn to tell the school rich girl that she's turning into the school creep?" Mary demanded.

"Who are you calling *creep?*" Lila shot back.

"You," Mary retorted.

"Stop it," I begged them both. "Stop acting like this." I felt a big lump rising in my throat. Seeing Lila revert like this was awful. She was being her old, spoiled, mean self. The Lila Fowler who only thought about Lila, who had never worked at the Center, thrown a party for disadvantaged kids, and learned to care about another person as much as she cared about herself.

She'd let somebody into her heart—and she'd gotten hurt. Now she was angry and determined to hurt everybody else. She was taking giant steps backward. And the worst part, judging from the look on Mary's face, was that she was taking the rest of us with her.

"Don't tell me what to do!" Lila shouted at me.

That's when Mrs. Arnette stuck her head out of her classroom and gave us a dirty look. "Girls," she said sharply. "Settle down and get to your classrooms."

"We're not doing anything wrong," Lila said in a snotty voice. Then, just to spite Mrs. Arnette, she slammed her locker shut and stalked off down the hall.

The sound reverberated all through the hall. And even when I had gone into my classroom, I still kept hearing it. Somehow, the sound of that locker slamming shut seemed like an omen to me.

"What's with Lila and Mary?" Jessica asked me after third period.

I was standing at my locker with Jessica and Ellen.

"They were both in my second-period class," Jessica went on, "and they sat on opposite sides of the room and wouldn't speak to each other."

"Lois Waller was acting all-important and Lila blew her off." Ellen sniffed. "For some reason, Mary stuck up for Lois."

I glared at Ellen. "Of course she stuck up for

Lois. Lila was being obnoxious," I said.

"What do you mean by that?" Jessica demanded. "We're a club. That means we stick up for each other no matter what."

"Even when one of us is wrong?" I asked.

"Yes," Jessica and Ellen said.

"No," I shot back.

"Look, don't get down on Lila. She's upset because of Ellie," Ellen said.

"We're all upset about Ellie," I argued. "That doesn't give us the right to be obnoxious. Does it?"

Jessica and Ellen stared back at me with stony faces.

"I think that friends are supposed to be loyal," Jessica said in a level tone.

I just shook my head and walked away. Whether we were Unicorns or not, right was right and wrong was wrong.

Wasn't it?

It made me think again about clubs. About friends. Most of all, it made me wonder about loyalty.

What did loyalty mean, really? It wasn't hard to be loyal to a friend or to a group when you were convinced that they were right. So maybe real loyalty was when you stuck by people even when you thought they were wrong.

I was sitting in the library after lunch, doing some research for my history paper, when Ms. Lustre, the librarian, tapped me on the shoulder.

"Go to Mr. Clark's office," she said in a curt voice.

"Mr. Clark's office? Now?"

She nodded. "His office just sent a student messenger to find you."

"Why?"

"I have no idea. All I know is that he's waiting for you, so you'd better hurry." Ms. Lustre went back to the stacks, and I picked up my books and shoved them into my backpack.

There had been a lump in my stomach ever since that scene this morning with Lila and the fight with Ellen and Jessica. Now it felt even heavier.

Somehow I just knew this wasn't good.

When I walked into Mr. Clark's office, I felt even more convinced that something was wrong—I just didn't know what. Jessica, Lila, Ellen, and Mary were already there, but their faces were carefully blank. Nobody was looking at anybody else.

"Sit down," Mr. Clark said, pointing to an empty chair beside Ellen.

I sat. Ellen gave me a scared look and then dropped her eyes to her feet.

Mr. Clark cleared his throat. "Some time ago, a stripe of wet purple paint appeared along a bank of lockers in the South Hall of the school." Mr. Clark clasped his hands behind his back and began pacing back and forth in front of us.

"Though I had my suspicions about who was responsible, I had no proof. Until today." He whirled around and fixed Ellen and Jessica with a glare. "As I was passing the lockers a few minutes ago, I observed Ellen and Jessica engaged in conversation beside Jessica's open locker. Inside that locker, and clearly visible from where I stood, was this."

He leaned over and picked something up from behind his desk.

Clank!

We all jumped in our seats.

There on his desk was one very small, very incriminating can of purple paint.

Mr. Clark sat down in his chair, picked up a pen, and tapped it thoughtfully against his desk. "I see nothing to be gained by suspending you girls from classes. But as we discussed, the Unicorn Club was already on probation. I'm afraid this is the final straw. I am declaring the Unicorn Club an illegal organization. Effective immediately."

We all gasped.

"From here on in, you are disbanded. You may no longer hold meetings, either on school property or off of it. For the next several weeks you may not congregate in groups of more than two. And you may not wear colors, jackets, hats, or any other insignia that might suggest official organization. Notes will go home to parents this afternoon asking for their cooperation."

It's times like these when you find out who your friends are.

Some people were really sympathetic when they found out the Unicorns had been declared an illegal organization. But some people acted as though we'd finally gotten what was coming to us. Some of the remarks people made really hurt my feelings.

"It's about time somebody broke them up," I overheard Randy Mason say to Peter DeHaven that afternoon in the library. "They've been practically running the school for as long as I've been here," he added.

I peeked through the books on the shelf and saw Randy and Peter sitting at a library table on the other side of the shelf. Caroline Pearce and Lois Waller were sitting there, too.

"I don't get it," Peter DeHaven said. "What exactly did Mr. Clark tell them?"

"He said they couldn't be a club anymore. They can't have meetings or congregate in groups of more than two," Caroline Pearce told them excitedly. She was leaning forward, filling them in as though she were the anchor on the six o'clock news. It made me want to throw a book at her. "He sent letters to all of their parents and a memo to all the teachers, asking them to help enforce the Unicorn ban. They're having a teachers' meeting about it this afternoon."

Good grief. I couldn't believe it. No wonder Caroline Pearce had such a reputation for being a gossip. The news was only about two and a half hours old and Caroline Pearce already knew more about it than we did.

"All I've got to say is *good riddance*," Lois said with a sigh. "By themselves, they're OK. But when they all get together, they're too obnoxious for words."

I felt my face flush. They were saying exactly what I had been thinking all along. But they were only partially right. The Unicorns all together could also be wonderful—capable of doing important and generous things.

OK. So Lila had been rude to Lois. She had been way out of line, and I didn't blame Lois for being mad at her. But Lila had been heartbroken over Ellie and obviously unable to say how she really felt. No, it didn't give her the right to be cruel. But couldn't Lois and the rest of them cut her any slack at all? Why did they only judge her by her faults and not by her good qualities? That was as bad as judging Lois by her weight and nothing else.

I remembered last year, when I had cancer. If it hadn't been for the Unicorns coming by and visiting me, I wouldn't have had any friends or any company. It wasn't as though Randy Mason, Peter DeHaven, or Lois Waller had come by to see me.

Why? Because they weren't Unicorns. They were nice kids. But they hadn't felt any particular sense of friendship or responsibility or loyalty to me.

The Unicorns were my friends. Without them, it was just . . . how had Elizabeth put it that afternoon at the Wakefields' pool? *"A pea rattling around in a great big pan with a thousand other peas. Not sure where I belong or how I fit in."* Something like that.

Maybe Jessica had been right. Friends were loyal no matter what.

No. I knew better than that. She was only half right. Loyalty didn't mean you said people were right even when they were wrong. Loyalty was when you knew they were wrong and weren't afraid to tell them so.

Loyalty was when you stayed their friend anyway and believed in their ability to do better next time.

"Mandy! Wait up."

I was walking home from school so lost in my own thoughts that I didn't even hear Elizabeth and Maria at first. My mind was just in a whirl. What was going to happen to all of us? If we couldn't be friends anymore, who were we supposed to hang out with? Talk to? Confide in?

I needed my friends. We all needed one another.

I heard footsteps behind me as Elizabeth and Maria came running to catch up with me.

"Wait!" Elizabeth called out again.

I whirled around and faced them. "If you're going to tell me you're glad about the Unicorns, please don't," I snapped.

Elizabeth's face fell. "I wasn't going to say that," she protested.

"Me neither," Maria added.

I lifted one eyebrow. "You might as well. I know you guys don't like the Unicorns and never have."

Elizabeth shifted her books from one hip to the other. "That's not true." She looked me right in the eye. "I don't feel that way anymore. In fact, I was beginning to think the Unicorns were pretty amazing. Mrs. Willard and the kids at the Center sure think you're great."

"It's really sad," Maria said, shaking her head. "Just when the Unicorns were doing some good, you guys get busted. I'm really going to be sorry to see you go."

I gave them a reluctant smile. "I don't think anybody else will. Especially not Mr. Clark. He thinks we're a bunch of useless snots."

Elizabeth looked at me, a thoughtful expression in her eyes. "There must be some way of changing his mind," she said. "We just have to think of what it is."

"We'll think of something," Maria said, putting her hand on my shoulder. "Somehow, between the three of us, I bet we can figure out a way to save the Unicorns."

"I think the thing that Mr. Clark and everybody else needs to know," Elizabeth said slowly, "is that the Unicorns have changed."

"You guys are illegal?" Archie demanded that evening while we were in the kitchen helping my mom fix dinner. "Wow! What did you do? Rob a bank or something?"

"We're not illegal," I corrected. "The club is illegal." Then I turned to my mom, who was standing at the sink washing spinach. "And Mr. Clark is wrong to bust us up." I sighed. "I wish you would write to him and tell him you don't approve of what he's doing."

Mom shook out the spinach and began tearing it up and dropping it into a bowl. "No. I can't. Because I do approve of what he's doing."

"Mom!"

"Vandalism. Rudeness. Pack behavior." She tore another spinach leaf. "This is not the kind of behavior I expect from my daughter." She wiped her hands on a dish towel and glared at me. "The note I'm sending Mr. Clark promises my full cooperation."

"Mom!"

"And after dinner, you can go right up to your room. Because you're grounded."

"Till when?"

"Until I decide you're not."

"Mom!"

"Mandy!"

"Wow!" Archie said.

After dinner I trudged upstairs to my room, hoping Maria and Elizabeth hadn't forgotten about us. Clearly, the Unicorns were going to need all the friends they could get.

Fourteen

"You haven't called Mrs. Willard to cancel?" I whispered.

Lila shook her head. "No," she whispered back. "I just can't bring myself to do it."

"The longer we wait, the worse it's going to be for them," Mary whispered.

It had been almost a week since Mr. Clark had banned the Unicorns, and we were all lined up at the water fountain, pretending we were waiting for a drink.

"Maybe Mr. Clark will change his mind about us and then we can keep our promise," Ellen said hopefully.

"*Girls!*"

We all looked up guiltily. Mr. Bowman was walking toward us. "Break it up," he directed.

"Mr. Bowman," Ellen whined, "we're just waiting for a drink of water."

I noticed Peter DeHaven and Rick Hunter were watching the scene with great interest from the doorway of the art room.

"You know the rules," Mr. Bowman said. "No congregating in groups of more than two."

We all sighed, and Peter and Rick began to snicker.

"I'm sorry, girls. My orders come from the top. Now break it up and get to class."

Lila and I left together since we had the next class together. "Listen, Lila," I said. "I'm going to the Center on Saturday to tell Mrs. Willard and the kids not to count on the kids' day at the zoo. It's not fair to let them get their hopes up for nothing."

"You're right," Lila agreed. "I'll meet you there and help you break it to them."

"You will?"

"Yeah," Lila said. "I hate doing it, but it has to be done." She cut her eyes to the side to make sure we weren't being overheard. "In fact, I think we should all meet there on Saturday."

"Lila!"

"I know we're not supposed to. But nobody will ever know. I'll put a note in everybody's locker."

"What a coincidence!" Elizabeth exclaimed that Saturday afternoon in a voice of comic surprise as I came into the playroom. Maria was there, too, and she began to laugh.

I saw that Mary, Jessica, and Ellen were already there.

They all giggled nervously. "Don't tell on us," Mary begged. "Please. We had something to tell the kids and we thought it was important that we all tell them together."

Elizabeth looked puzzled, but before we could explain about the zoo, the door burst open and Lila came running in all excited and out of breath.

"Where's Mrs. Willard? Where is she?"

"What's wrong?" we all demanded.

"Nothing's wrong," Lila said happily. "Something's right. Something's wonderful."

"Did I hear someone call my name?" Mrs. Willard asked, appearing at the door. Then she frowned. "Girls, I hate to be a spoilsport, but according to Mr. Clark, you're not supposed to be here as a group."

"Oh, Mrs. Willard," Lila begged. "Please don't make us leave. I have some news. And I want everybody to hear it."

She stopped to catch her breath as we all came over.

"I just talked to my dad," she said with a happy smile. "And guess what? *He found Mrs. McMillan a job!*"

All of us jumped into the air, screaming and shouting and pumping our fists. Even the kids were jumping around laughing—and I'm not really sure they knew what was going on.

"Daddy said something opened up in the downtown office," Lila went on. "And he said Mrs. McMillan would be perfect. If you'll give me her phone number, I'll call my dad and he'll call her today." She grinned. "I can't wait to see Ellie's face when we tell her."

There was a long silence and Mrs. Willard's face looked stricken. "Oh, dear. I'm afraid I don't have her phone number. All I know is that she's somewhere in Los Angeles."

Lila's face fell. "What about Ellie? Where is she? You must know where she's living!" Lila's voice was rising to a dangerous pitch of frustration.

Mrs. Willard shook her head again. "I don't know that either, dear. People often remove their children from the Center and don't necessarily tell us where they're going. All I know is that she placed Ellie in foster care and went to Los Angeles to look for work."

"This is terrible!" Lila choked.

I put my arm around her shoulders. "I'm sorry," I said softly.

The Wild Bunch had gathered around us and they looked so worried when they saw Lila crying.

"What's the matter with her?" Oliver asked me in a whisper.

"She's sad," Jessica answered.

"Why is she sad?" Allison asked.

"Because she misses Ellie," Mary said.

"Ohhhhh." Sandy nodded. "We're sad, too."

Their heads moved solemnly up and down, and Yuky's thumb disappeared into her mouth as she appeared to be thinking hard.

"Maybe we should look for her," Ellen suggested.

"Where?" Jessica said. "Sweet Valley is big. It could take us twenty years to ring every doorbell in town."

I shook my head. It was just horrible. Here was the happy ending. Right there in sight. And it wasn't going to happen, because Ellie and Mrs. McMillan had disappeared. Vanished. Lost out there in the great big world with millions of other people. People who had no connection to Mrs. McMillan. Or Ellie. Or the Unicorns. Or even to one other.

Something plucked at my sleeve and I opened my eyes. It was Yuky. She waggled her finger, signaling me to bend down.

"What is it?" I asked, squatting down so that we were face to face. "Do you want to go to the bathroom?"

She didn't nod. She didn't smile. She didn't even blink. She just opened her mouth. "I know where Ellie is," she answered in a tiny, breathless whisper.

I almost fell over. I couldn't believe it. I guess Yuky saved her words for critical situations.

Everybody immediately squatted down, surrounding Yuky and leaning forward to catch her words. Yuky put her thumb back in her mouth and shrank a little against my arm.

"Shhhh," I warned everybody. "Don't scare her." I turned back to Yuky. "Tell me where you think Ellie is, OK?" I coaxed.

Yuky smiled but she kept working on the thumb.

Gently, I removed the thumb and asked her the question again.

"I heard her mommy talking on the telephone," she whispered. "She said Ellie would be living on, um, South Elm Street." She stuck her thumb back in her mouth.

"South Elm," Mary said. "I know where that is. It's in the Ridgedale section. My old piano teacher lived there."

"What are we waiting for?" Lila said excitedly. "Let's go!"

"Girls," Mrs. Willard called out. "Wait. Mr. Clark said—"

But we were already on our way out the door.

"We'll call you when we find her," Jessica called out.

"Ellie!" I cried.

"Ellie, where are you?" Jessica and Mary shouted on the other side of the block.

It was getting late and we had been combing the Ridgedale section for over an hour, going up and down each block, looking for tricycles or toys in the yard. Anything that indicated there were kids inside.

We rang lots of door bells and stopped everybody we saw on the street. But nobody seemed to know anything about Ellie or Mrs. McMillan.

"Maybe we should call it quits for today," Jessica said as we all met at the end of the block. "It's going to be dark soon and . . ."

She broke off and her eyes focused on something in the distance. "Hey! Look down there."

We all looked in the direction of her pointing finger. There was a park on the other side of the intersection—a tiny neighborhood park. "Come on," she said. "Let's check it out."

The next thing we knew, we were all running. It was our last hope.

And believe it or not, when we came around the corner, we spotted a familiar little brunette head.

"*Ellie!*" Lila shouted.

She was swinging on the swing set. And when she spotted us, she kicked her heels with joy and swung high up against the blue sky with a happy shriek. "Unicorns!"

When she'd stopped her swing, she jumped off and ran toward Lila with her arms opened wide.

Lila opened her own arms and swept her up in a hug. And pretty soon the rest of us were all huddled together, with our arms around Ellie, Lila, and one another.

A very nice-looking lady with a long red braid looked very confused until we explained who we were. It turned out she was Ellie's foster mom. Her name was Mrs. Conwell, and she lived just down the block.

When we told her about finding a job for Mrs. McMillan, she invited us right back to the house to call. She had Mrs. McMillan's number and knew she'd be thrilled to hear from us.

As soon as we got to the house, Mrs. Conwell got Mrs. McMillan on the phone and then put Lila on.

"Mrs. McMillan," Lila said breathlessly. "Pack your bags and come back to Sweet Valley."

She broke into a broad grin and smiled at all of us as she listened to the excited chatter on the other end of the line.

"That's right. My dad found you a job. He says you can start on Monday."

We all tried to get as close to the receiver as possible so we could hear what she was saying. But there were too many of us to get our ears close enough.

"What is she saying?" Mary hissed.

"She said she'd start driving back tonight. And then she just started crying," Lila told us, starting to cry, too.

And you know what? After that we *all* started crying. Even Mrs. Conwell.

That night, I was lying in the bathtub thinking about what had happened that afternoon.

By Monday, Ellie would be back at the Center. Mrs. McMillan would be at her new job. A family would be reunited—and it would all be because of us.

Could a club that cared that much really be as awful as Mr. Clark seemed to think? No. And Mr. Clark needed to hear the truth.

That's when I remembered Elizabeth and Maria. They had said they wanted to help. If they were serious, maybe they could.

Because as I was scrubbing my back, I came up with a great idea.

"That's a great idea," Elizabeth said later over the phone. "A petition would probably do a lot of good."

"Think Maria will go for it?" I asked.

"I know she will," Elizabeth assured me. "Especially when she hears the story about Ellie and Mrs. McMillan, I know we can count on her help. I'll tell you what. I'll write the petition tonight, and then I'll go over to the Center tomorrow morning and get Mrs. Willard and the staff to sign it."

"Thanks, Elizabeth," I said. "You may not be a Unicorn, but you're an awesome friend."

Monday was the longest day of my whole life. I didn't tell any of my friends what Elizabeth and Maria and I had planned. Elizabeth and Maria might not have been able to find Mrs. Willard. Sometimes she wasn't at the Center until late in the day. And I didn't want to disappoint them if the thing didn't come off.

But it was hard not to tell them. We needed some feeling of hope.

Because of our dare war, I guess, we were not exactly the most popular girls in school. The teachers were mad at us, the administration was mad at us, and most of the students were mad at us. We were forbidden to speak to one another, so as you can imagine, school days were long and lonely.

Even wearing my favorite hat that day—the one with the big silk flower on the brim—didn't cheer me up.

All things considered, the prognosis wasn't too good. Even if Maria and Elizabeth did get a petition from the Center, it probably wouldn't carry much weight. After all, there were only a few employees there besides Mrs. Willard. What would a few signatures mean compared with an entire middle-school student body that seemed to hate us?

Maybe Maria and Elizabeth had come to that same conclusion. Maybe they hadn't even tried. Maybe they'd figured it was just a waste of time to get into a big argument with Mr. Clark over the Unicorns. I tried not to underestimate Elizabeth and Maria. But who could blame them? After all, it wasn't their club.

I was on the verge of tears when the final bell rang. Students began pouring out of the classrooms and streaming into the halls.

Randy Mason was just ahead of me when suddenly he stopped.

"What's that noise?" he asked.

In the background, behind the din of banging

lockers and laughing kids, I heard a low, steady droning noise. It sounded like chanting.

"There's a demonstration outside!" Peter De-Haven shouted from the other end of the hall.

"A demonstration?" I squeaked. Immediately, I began pushing my way through the hall.

The hallway had erupted into excited chatter, and all the kids were hurrying to the front doors of the building to see what was going on.

I was in the back of the crowd when I heard the group at the front burst into laughter.

"What's going on?" I heard Mary ask.

Ellen, who was just ahead of her, shrugged. "I can't see."

"What is that chanting?" Jessica shouted at us from the other side of the crowd.

I strained my ears to hear and finally was able to make out the words.

"Save the Unicorns! Save the Unicorns!"

Mary turned and grabbed my sleeve. "Come on!" she urged, yanking me forward through the crowd.

"Save the Unicorns!" the crowd chanted as they marched up to the front door of the school.

I couldn't believe what I saw.

It really was a demonstration. Elizabeth and Maria were at the front of the crowd. Behind them marched Mrs. McMillan and Ellie, Mrs. Willard, Arthur Foo, Mr. and Mrs. Foo, Oliver and Mr. Johnson, Sandy and Allison Meyer and their mom, and Yuky, followed by both her parents and all five of her brothers and sisters. The group carried a long banner on which they had lettered the words SAVE THE UNICORNS!

When they saw us come through the door, they all looked up and waved. Tears ran down my cheeks as I waved back.

I should never have doubted Elizabeth and Maria. They hadn't bothered with a puny little petition. They had put together a whole demonstration. And no doubt about it, it was impressive.

I held my breath when I saw Mr. Clark appear. He was clearly wondering what all the commotion was about. I was worried he was going to explode. But when he saw the demonstration, I swear the corners of his mouth began to twitch.

Mrs. Willard stepped to the front of the group and held up her hands for quiet. "If I could have your attention for just a moment, I'd like to say a word on behalf of the Unicorns."

Everybody quieted right down.

"Perhaps the students and faculty of Sweet Valley Middle School are unaware that Unicorns are among the rarest and most special creatures on the planet. Unicorns are strong and loyal. Best of all, for this group of children at least, they made wishes come true."

I felt chills skate down my spine as I watched everyone listening. And I could feel their eyes on us as Mrs. Willard told them about all the things we had done. How we'd rescued the cat and one of the kids during the storm. How we'd given the kids a day they would never forget. And how we'd kept a family—Mrs. McMillan and Ellie—together.

"And so," she finished, "on behalf of the Sweet Valley Child Care Center, we ask that Sweet Valley Middle School"—she turned around and motioned to the rest of the demonstrators—"save the Unicorns!" they all shouted together.

There was a long pause.

Then, finally, Lois Waller lifted her fist. "Save the Unicorns!" she shouted.

"Save the Unicorns!" Caroline Pearce, Brooke Dennis, Melissa McCormick, and Julie Porter joined in.

"Save the Unicorns!" the whole school shouted. I noticed that Mrs. Arnette, Mr. Bowman, and several other teachers had joined in.

Mr. Clark stepped through the crowd toward where the protesters stood. He lifted his hands, signaling everyone to settle down.

As the crowd grew quiet again, he looked from the demonstrators to us. "In the face of such overwhelming support," he said. "I think my duty is clear. The ban is lifted."

I threw my hat up in the air, then threw my arms around Jessica. Lila threw her arms around the two of us, and pretty soon, the whole club was in a huddle.

"Long live the Unicorns!" we shouted.

Fifteen

"OK," Lila said. "I've lined up the stretch limo to take us all to the zoo tomorrow. We've got permission slips from all the parents. I think that just about wraps it up."

Everybody applauded, and Lila sat back down on the comfortable couch in the Wakefields' living room.

It was our first official Unicorn meeting since the ban had been lifted, and most of the meeting had been taken up with planning the trip to the zoo the following day and trying to come up with ways to make money. Mr. Clark had lifted the ban, but we still owed him money for his toupee, and he was still going to make us pay to have the lockers repainted.

We had solved all the logistical problems about the kids' day at the zoo, and we had come up with a long list of money-making ideas.

But we still didn't have a president. Every time the question was raised for discussion, it got shoved to the back burner. I think it was a painful subject. After all, picking a president was what had started all our problems.

But a club needed to have a president. Somebody to lead us. Somebody to keep us moving in the right direction. We'd learned how easy it was to get off on the wrong track.

It was time somebody took the Unicorn by the horn. I cleared my throat and stood. "I think it's time to have an honest discussion about the club. Who we are and where we're going."

Everybody sighed.

"I agree," Mary said. She took a big handful of salt-and-vinegar potato chips out of a bowl, and then started the bowl around the room. "We've changed in the last few weeks, and I'm glad. I feel more comfortable being a Unicorn this year than I did last year, in spite of all the problems we've had lately."

"We've always had a reputation for being the prettiest and most popular girls at school. And that's great. But we've also had a reputation for being really snobby. And that's not so great," Ellen said. She passed the bowl of chips to Lila.

"I never realized how much people resented us until we were banned," Lila said thoughtfully, staring down into the bowl.

"Me either," Jessica piped in.

"So where do we go from here?" Mary asked. "What kind of club do we want to be?"

"I think the thing to remember," I said tentatively, "is that Janet Howell isn't here anymore. It's our club now. We can make our club whatever we want it to be."

"But what do we want it to be?" Ellen asked.

Every eye was on me—as though they were waiting to hear what else I had to say.

I cleared my throat. "The kind of club that brings out the best in its members, not the worst," I said slowly.

There was a long silence while that sank in.

"Works for me," Lila said finally, nodding her head.

"Me, too," Mary said.

"Me, three," Jessica chimed in.

"Me, four." Ellen smiled.

"Me, five," I said, sitting down with a sigh. I was incredibly relieved to have that settled. "So now all we have to do is pick a president."

"I nominate Mandy Miller," Jessica said quickly. *What?*

"I second the nomination," Lila said immediately.

"All in favor," Mary said.

"Aye!" the four of them shouted.

"Why me?" I gasped. I couldn't believe it. I'd never even considered it.

"Because you're the one who always sees the best in us," Mary said.

Everybody nodded.

"So will you be our president?" Ellen asked.

"Come on, Mandy. You can't say no," Jessica said.

What could I say? I'd been drafted. Suckered. Shanghaied. But I couldn't think of a bigger honor in the world. "You bet," I said happily.

I heard laughter outside, and I looked up and saw Elizabeth and Maria Slater in the pool again. Hmmmm.

All of a sudden I had an idea. But I wasn't sure how far my presidential powers extended. Janet Howell had ruled with an iron hand. I was the one talking about a kinder, gentler club. Still, my idea was a good one—so I decided to try it out.

I stood up and turned my baseball hat backward on my head. "As my first official act as president, I'd like to propose two new members. Elizabeth Wakefield and Maria Slater. If it weren't for them, we wouldn't be a club anymore. We'd still be an illegal organization."

Everybody looked surprised.

Amazed.

Jessica's mouth was open in shock.

"What if they don't want to join?" Mary finally asked. "Don't forget, Elizabeth was invited to join last year and she said no."

"That was then and this is now." I smiled. "And I also propose a new motto. *Nothing ventured, nothing gained.*"

*   *   *

"Look out!" Oliver shouted—just two seconds too late.

Phtooo!

"Gross!" Lila groaned, jumping back from the baby camel.

"I told you," Oliver said with a laugh. "They spit."

The rest of the Wild Bunch burst into delighted giggles.

Lila picked Ellie up. "Camels are just too rude. Let's find some animals with better manners."

"Let's go see the pigs!" Sandy shouted, leading our whole group toward the next pen, which was full of adorable pink baby pigs.

So far, the kids' day was turning out to be a total success. And our two newest Unicorns, Elizabeth and Maria, were having the best time of all.

"I'm so glad you and Maria decided to join," I said with a smile as Elizabeth stepped between Arthur Foo and an overly friendly pig.

"Me, too," Elizabeth said. "It was a big decision for me. I hope I made the right one."

Mary came running over to us. "I just checked the prices at the refreshment stand. Popsicles are a dollar apiece. Do we have enough in the treasury?"

I stuck my hand in my pocket and pulled out all that remained of our club dues. "We've got just enough for a Popsicle apiece. So let's be sure they don't drop them. We can't afford replacements." I handed Mary the money and she ran off to get the Popsicles.

"Looks like this is our last Unicorn outing for a while." I sighed. "From now on, we've got to concentrate our funds on paying Mr. Clark back for his toupee and covering the cost of painting the lockers."

"Why don't we offer to paint the lockers ourselves?" Elizabeth suggested. "That way we would only have to pay for the paint. It couldn't be that expensive."

"That's a good idea," I said. "Just don't let Jessica pull her Tom Sawyer picket fence routine on you."

Elizabeth rolled her eyes. "Don't worry. I know all Jessica's tricks."

"Even if we do paint the lockers ourselves, we've still got to raise some major bucks to replace Mr. Clark's hairpiece. But I think I have an idea about that. You know that new thrift store on Mill Street?"

She nodded.

"I've been in there two or three times and the lady who owns it told me she has to go away on business for a couple of weeks. That means she's got to hire somebody to run the store in the afternoon."

"And you think we should apply for the job?"

I nodded. "We're not really old enough to work there, but I bet if we volunteered she'd be willing to pay us at least a little."

Thrift stores happen to be my personal all-time favorite places to hang out. And the idea of getting to hang out in one for possible profit as well as fun was totally exciting.

"That sounds like fun," Elizabeth said with a grin. "When can we start?"

And that's how our thrift-store adventure started. But hey, I've been hogging the floor. I'll let somebody else tell you that story.

Read all about the Unicorns' next adventure in The Unicorn Club #2, MARIA'S MOVIE COMEBACK.